THE HEART OF A WESTSIDE MOB BOSS

SHONTAIYE MOORE

COPYRIGHT

INTRODUCTION

Fourteen. That's the age I gave birth to my son. Shit, I had no idea I was even pregnant until I fainted in math class one day and woke up with the school nurse kneeling over me.

"Easton sweetie, you fainted. Just stay down for now, until help gets here. You're going to the hospital so we can have you checked out."

Judging by the mob of teachers and other staff that were crowded around me, I'd been out for a while. I blinked my eyes and looked at the nurse in confusion. My legs had been propped up and her white ass kept asking me questions and reassuring me that I would be okay. Something was definitely wrong. I felt funny and I'd been feeling that way for nearly a week. I was exhausted and my head was doing a slow spin. Thankfully, it didn't take long for a couple of paramedics to show up and whisk me away in an ambulance.

After I arrived, the doctors ran a series of tests and not long after, I was given the shocking news that I was preg-

nant. An hour later, I had a case manager all up in my damn face asking me a bunch of questions. Imagine being told that you're pregnant after having sex for the first time only a few months before. It was a lot to take in. They didn't even give me time to digest the information. Just question after question.

"Did you know you were pregnant?"

That was one of the first questions, and the one that annoyed me most. Of course, I didn't know. I'd just lost my virginity to a nigga from my neighborhood named Ray-Ray, who'd been pushing up on me for months. Everybody knew I was the neighborhood virgin. As crazy as it may have seemed, I was literally one of the last virgins left. Most of the girls I knew had been fucking since they were eleven and twelve, but I'd held out until I was thirteen. Where I was from, that was an accomplishment.

Did you know you were pregnant? The question echoed in my ears. Laying in the hospital bed, I shook my head in response to the nosey bitch's question.

"No, I didn't know. I would've said that shit in the beginning."

I rolled my eyes at her in her tight suit and stiff ass wig. Rolling over to my side, I gave that case manager my back to look at.

"Are you or is there any chance that you may be pregnant?"

I'd told them no, and that was the God's honest truth. I wasn't trying to get snappy; I just wanted her to stop asking me stupid ass shit.

"Do you know who the father is?" she continued, unbothered by my rudeness.

I frowned and gave her a blank stare to hide my increasing irritation. Ray-Ray had just turned eighteen years old. I was jailbait and outside of the neighborhood, no one was supposed to know about us. What was acceptable in the hood, oftentimes wasn't acceptable outside of it. Telling people that I was thirteen years old and involved with an eighteen-year-old was a surefire way to get him scooped up by the police. It was a small world, and West Baltimore was even smaller. Somebody knew somebody so I refused to even utter his name out of fear that I'd get my man in a heap of trouble.

"Yeah," I said quickly, turning my gaze from her to the floor. "I know who the father is, but who he is, ain't none of yo' business."

The news. The hospital. The nurses. I would remember that day. Remember my words. I'd stood on them and refused to answer any questions about Ray-Ray. If he got caught up behind me, who would be there to help take care of our child? I was so fucking young and delusional, thinking that he and I would be together forever. That we would raise our baby and live happily ever after. Wrong as ever! I should had told that bitch everything I knew. Ray-Ray ugly ass dipped on me before my belly could swell. Said 'to hell' with us. That was my very first experience with a fuck nigga and I vowed to make it my last.

Fourteen years old with a damn baby. What the hell was I going to do? I had no real help. My mom was a drunk and the man that was supposed to be my daddy was in jail. Two worthless motherfuckers that barely took care of me and my sister. Because of my age, I couldn't get any assistance unless my mom got off her ass. But I knew that would never happen. She was so lazy that she didn't even bother to add my baby to her food stamp case. Refusing to depend on her, I had to make shit happen for my damn self.

My son, Dayquan Blue, was my first true love. I gave him my last name because I'd gouge my eyes out with scissors before I honored a wack ass nigga that I knew wasn't about to do shit for my baby. Still young and dumb, but still smart enough to know that I wasn't running behind no nigga.

The moment Quan came screaming into the world, I vowed to do my best. I became a protector, and I took motherhood seriously. My boy depended on me, and I had to make sure his needs were met. I started hustling at fourteen. Doing hair that is. Whatever I could make to keep clothes on my baby's back and food in his belly. I would do anything for my son and sixteen years later; after living for him, I would be forced to learn to live without him.

EASTON BLUE

"**S**o that's what we doing now?" I asked my man Zalo the moment he walked into the bedroom we shared.

I had been lying in bed, but as soon as he came through the door, I jumped up. Barefoot, and practically naked in a bra and panties, I stood there with a bright, purple bonnet on my head, arms tucked into one another, waiting for him to explain himself. His eyes met mine briefly before he quickly looked away.

"Please don't start," he huffed, as he began carefully removing his jewelry and clothing.

"It's four in the fuckin' morning Zalo. Why wouldn't I start?" I hissed, my eyes shooting daggers.

Zalo averted his gaze and continued to focus on undressing. Carefully placing his chain and diamond medallion onto the dresser, he then removed his Rolex watch. He tossed his orange Nike Tech suit on the accent chair in the corner of the room. The sight of his slim but defined body intensified my anger. He was supposed to be all mine. Literally and figuratively. We'd exchanged vows and signed papers. Yet I was sharing his heart and his body with a wanna-be Instagram bitch.

Zalo was undeniably sexy. Tall, dark-chocolate skin with a faded low Caesar cut, and a dick that curved, he was on every ghetto bitch's wish list. I remembered when I'd first laid eyes on him, my cousin had to nearly push my lips together. I could practically taste him. Pretty, ivory-colored teeth that looked like they'd been straightened by the best orthodontist in the city. The man could literally have any hoe he wanted in the 410 and 443 area code. Myself included.

I was doing my best to contain my anger, but Zalo wasn't making that easy. The disregard and nonchalance that he displayed, indicated that he didn't give a fuck about my feelings nor what I was talking about. Now standing in just his Ethika boxers and socks, he hadn't responded; instead, he sighed as if he didn't want to be bothered. As if I was the one who was the problem.

"You really wanna do this Easton?" he questioned, finally turning his gaze to me.

The look he gave me was intense, challenging and questioning.

"What the fuck ever Za," I said knowing where he was headed.

I blew out a frustrated breath, disconnected my

arms and called myself backing out of the argument, but Zalo had other plans.

"Na, it ain't no '*whatever*'. This was *your* decision, remember?" he reminded me.

"No. It wasn't my decision. It was a solution to your problem," I countered.

He cocked his head to the side in disbelief, eyeing me like I had two heads.

"*My problem?* More like, *your* problem." He scoffed. "Let's go there, E."

My assumption that he didn't want to argue was wrong. The way his words came out were confrontational. Like he had something to say. Like he'd been wanting to get some shit off his chest for a while.

"You know what … it's too late for this shit. Do what the fuck you want, but don't be in your feelings when I do the same."

I continued to stand in the middle of the room, giving Zalo a daring look. He knew I wasn't the one to fuck with. I was in a vulnerable state and in a sense, I felt like I was being kicked while I was down. I wasn't proud of it, but I could be vindictive at times. Anyone that fucked me, got fucked back extra hard.

"Get smacked, talkin' stupid," he threatened, his lip curling upward into a snarl. "It was *you* who told me to go out and fuck other bitches because you weren't in the mental space to fuck me. I only did what you told me to do."

His snarl had turned into an incredulous look.

"Go out and *fuck* other bitches!" I countered, the volume in my voice increasing.

I quickly checked myself. We lived in a luxury apartment and although it was big, I didn't want any of our conversation being heard by anyone else.

"My words were, '*go out and get what you need until I can give it to you again*'. I said *go fuck*, not go out and fuck the same bitch over and over. Or fall the fuck in love. And I definitely didn't give yo' ass permission to come waltzing up in this bitch at four in the fuckin' morning!" I yelled again, this time getting all up in his face and mushing his forehead with my finger.

"I don't need permission to do shit," he countered before extending his arm. "Back the fuck up," he demanded, gently pushing me with the palm of his hand.

I went back a few steps, titties bouncing in my bra as I moved.

"And what I tell you about all that fuckin' noise with Ky in here? You loud enough for the neighbors to hear us, so I know damn well she can too."

"You forget that its four in the fuckin' morning. She sleep nigga!" I spat.

Zalo walked around me and climbed into bed.

"I know it's the same bitch because she makes it a priority to sneak diss on social media," I continued to argue. "You need to check that bitch, or I will," I argued, disregarding everything he said about the noise level.

I cared but then again, I didn't because I was angry.

4

"Yo, you not done?" he asked. "Come the fuck to bed," Zalo demanded, sliding under the sheets and getting comfortable.

Based on his tone and facial expressions, he was back to being completely unbothered by any of the shit I was saying. His audacity was at an all-time high.

"Fuck you, nigga. I'm going to sleep on the couch."

I was disgusted and I didn't want to be next to him, let alone lay up underneath the trifling nigga with his arm wrapped around me like shit was all good. The fucking around part didn't faze me. I couldn't meet his needs and fucking was merely transactional. But his ass was carrying on a whole affair and that did something to my soul, considering everything that I was going through. Yeah, I'd shut him out, but that was a normal response for anyone dealing with grief or a traumatic event. I still needed him and his way of being there was to go and have a whole affair with a bitch that made it known every other day.

I was about to turn around and head out of the room, but Zalo kicked the sheets off of him and jumped out of bed. He walked over to the accent chair where his clothes lay and began getting dressed.

"Where the fuck you going?" I asked.

"I'm not for none of that shit," he said impatiently. "You won't fuck me and now I can't even hold you after a long ass day. You rather waste time arguing." He shook his head. "The fuck I come home for?" he asked as if he was truly expecting an answer.

He looked at me with bewilderment. When I didn't answer, he kept running his mouth.

"I'm gon' crash over my ma's until you get your shit together."

My jaws clenched as I became overwhelmed with emotions. Tears threatened to spill from my eyes. It was a mixture of anger and hurt. I'd been through so much shit over the last year and as usual Zalo had turned something else into my fault. The way I saw it, I was being selfless letting him fuck around. But for God's sake, we were still married. Partnership was about sacrifice and I was sacrificing so he wouldn't have to. But now, he was straight up hurting me. I loved Zalo and I wanted him home, but the bitch Lola that he was fucking, was really starting to get under my skin.

This wasn't the first time that I'd argued with him about the shit she did on social media. Despite her disrespect, he kept fuckin' with her, so it made sense for me to take my anger out on him. It was about more than her subtle taunts; it was the fact that he was spending way too much time with the bitch. *Did he love her? Was he really going to his mom's house or was he going back to that bitch?*

"Do whatever the fuck you want," I said, pretending not to give a fuck, but deep down, my heart was screaming in agony.

I swallowed my cries. It was what I did best. Bottled up my emotions. That's what I'd been trained to do my whole life. Where I was from, that was expected of women. I walked back to bed and got in it while Zalo continued standing near the accent chair. He had his pants in his hand, but he put them down and instead eyed me intensely. I had no doubt that he could see right through my facade. After a few seconds, he shook his head.

"Look at you. Always running around like you so fuckin' tough," he said, shaking his head as if he pitied me. "Stop saying shit you don't mean. You don't really want me to go," he continued.

I didn't respond, nor did I bother to look at him when he talked.

"But I'm gonna go anyway. You don't really want me fuckin' other bitches, but you shut me out so I'm gonna keep doing that too, because what the fuck else can I do? You gotta fix the issues E. When you're ready, you let me know. Then it'll end."

He said it like the shit was so easy. Like I had the magic potion to fix what was going on inside of me. Zalo finished dressing, and without putting any of his jewelry back on, he disappeared back out the door he'd just walked through five minutes before.

After hearing the front door of the apartment shut, I tucked myself into the sheets and pulled the covers around me. Less than ten seconds later, my eyes had swelled. Another two seconds and the levee immediately broke, releasing all the tears behind it. I hated to admit it, but the space me and Zalo were in was my fault. Ever since Quan's death, I hadn't been the same. I'd literally transformed into a different person. I used to be fun, carefree and loving, but after that day ... It was like my light had been switched from bright to dark.

Gonzalo, aka. "Zalo" was a well-known dope dealer in the city. He along with a few others distributed to sections of West Baltimore and Southeast Baltimore, namely Highlandtown. Black and Hispanic because of his Puerto Rican mother, Zalo identified as both so he was able to work with the Hispanic dudes that were slinging dope in the city. It was a special market that most of the blacks couldn't touch.

Gonzalo was charming, handsome, and paid. We met at the Annual Parade of Latino Nations in Highlandtown. Bored with my cousin, we'd gone out to watch, and as two of the only Black girls there, we stuck out. My cousin Miracle, with her smooth chocolate skin and stallion-like physique, had that around-the-way-girl beauty. I, on the other hand, had been told I had more "exotic" features: golden-brown skin, full lips, slightly slanted eyes, and a head full of ringlet curls. I knew I was something special. Though I carried a little extra weight, I was blessed that none of it showed in my face. With high cheekbones and a chiseled yet feminine jawline, I had the kind of features chicks spent hours contouring to achieve. When Zalo and I locked eyes, he walked right over, and we hit it off immediately. Since that day, we had been inseparable.

After a few months of dating, I fell pregnant. Fast-forward, with Quan by our side, and our newly created baby girl, we became a family. We vowed to always remain a team, and we were happy ... until my son died in a car accident.

Grief was like the devil. It had taken over my soul. Tricked my brain and lied to me. It told me that I wasn't worthy of life. That I should just end it all. It told me not to eat. Not to bathe. To mistreat my daughter. Withhold my love from her and her father. I was lashing out at people, invalidating their pain because theirs was nowhere close to what I was feeling. My relationships with people took a hit.

It had been a little over a year since my son passed and Zalo and I had only had sex a handful of times. I just wasn't there and couldn't engage emotionally or physically. My mind was telling me I didn't deserve such pleasure. I felt guilty for even thinking to make that a priority.

Zalo urged me to see a therapist and I did, but the white bitch they'd connected me with was no help, so I stopped going. It got to the point that we began to argue about the lack of intimacy in our relationship. That's when I told him to *"do him"* until I was in the mental space to be with him. That was six months ago, and those words were coming back to bite me in the ass.

I loved my husband, and it hurt to know that there was a possibility that he could have feelings for someone else. I expected him to be discreet and at first, he was, but then I heard the name Lola.

I would never have known about their relationship

if Lola hadn't started posting all over social media. Instagram, Snap, and Facebook. Pictures of her riding shotgun in his car. Videos of expensive dinner dates. Day trips out of town. Zalo's face was never in the videos or pictures but motherfuckers that knew us, knew he was the mystery man. That's when people started going to my people and they started coming to me.

Zalo was well known in the city. His name rang like that and if you knew him or knew of him, you knew that he drove a cherry red Audi. My sister and my best friend Tyra had argued with me about things Lola had posted. The things they had heard and been approached with. Like it was my fault that I was allowing it. That I should put a stop to it. But how? I had no real proof, and he denied being the man that Lola was posting about and taking pictures with. Then came the 'you told me to do me' shit. It was hard to argue with Zalo when I had actually told him that fucking on other bitches until I was in a better space was cool.

The people that loved me and knew what was going on didn't care about the agreement. They felt that what she was doing was disrespectful. It didn't matter that she didn't post his face. Sometimes it would be his shoes, or his hand, or a hat in the fuckin' corner. The bitch wanted so bad to be relevant. She'd even gone as far as posting captions with her pictures that seemed like sneak disses to me. Shit like, *"His #1" "Daddy's favorite girl."* Or the kicker, *"She could never be me."*

I'd addressed the Lola shit with Zalo once, and I didn't expect to have to say anything else about it. The posts had slowed down, but they hadn't stopped and Zalo bringing his black ass in the house at four in the morning, was just another form of disrespect. I had no doubt he was with Lola, but what the fuck could I really argue? I couldn't fuck him, and somebody had to do the job. Right?

~

ornings. I squinted as bright sunlight poured in through the curtains. I groaned and pulled the comforter over my head. Most people welcomed the mornings. It was synonymous with second chances, fresh starts, and additional days granted by God. Naturally, I was thankful; yet as grateful as I was, I loathed them. Being able to open my eyes another day was a blessing, but it was also a reminder that my son wasn't able to do the same. It was hard to be happy when that was a constant in my thoughts.

"Hey Mommy."

Kyllie Megan Alvarez's voice filled my ears. She was so close that I knew that I could reach out and touch her. She was the beautiful reminder that I still had something to live for. Even though, it sure didn't feel like it.

"Good morning," I said after pulling the covers down from over my head.

She stood to my left, less than a foot away by the nightstand. Two rows of teeth proudly on display. My daughter was beautiful. A creamy tan complexion like her fathers, with strikingly similar features, she was absolutely adorable. Staring at her, a smile slowly began to stretch across my face. She was like the sun shining through the layers of darkness covering me.

Kyllie turned four in May, and she knew well enough not to disturb me while I was sleeping. She also knew that as soon as I cracked my damn eyes open, I was technically up, and boy did she take advantage of that shit. The moment she saw me stir and my eyes flutter open, she began asking questions and politely demanding shit.

"Good morning Mommy. Can you make me some pancakes?"

I was proud that she spoke so well, but I wasn't happy to hear her request. Although, I knew that it was coming. I briefly tore my eyes away from my daughter to my phone on the nightstand. I reached over and grabbed it. After pressing down on the side, the screen lit up and confirmed the time. 8:17 am. I sighed and closed my eyes back.

I knew that it was going to be early as fuck. It was still early for me, and that didn't have shit to do with me being up 'til nearly five in the morning arguing with Zalo's ass.

"Mommy," Kyllie said again, this time a tad bit more softly. "You make me some pancakes?"

She knew I didn't like getting up in the morning but

12

as a toddler she automatically placed her needs before anyone else's. And rightfully so.

"Mommy, I'm hungry," she continued a few seconds later, after not hearing a response.

My eyes were still closed. All I needed was just one more minute, but I knew I wasn't going to get it. About ten seconds later, Kyllie reached out and gently tapped my shoulder."

"Yes! I'm gonna make you some pancakes," I finally replied irritably as I lifted my upper body from the bed.

My tone was harsh, and my volume had been louder than what she was accustomed to. I immediately felt bad.

"Ky, can you just give me a minute to get up?" I asked, rubbing my eyes.

I was still irritated but my tone had softened. Regardless of the fact, the emotional damage had been done.

"I'm sorry Mommy," she said, her eyes widening slightly and her hands clasping together.

Her reaction broke my heart instantly. Kyllie was naturally energetic and talkative, but her voice had gotten smaller just that moment. She had been excited about those pancakes, but I'd taken that joy away. I felt like a piece of shit. I had to get it together and fucking fast. I inhaled wearily and then exhaled a deep breath.

"No. Don't be sorry. You did nothing wrong, so you have nothing to apologize for. Mommy's the one who is sorry."

Literally and figuratively were my thoughts.

"I got frustrated and I took that out on you," I continued. "You didn't deserve that," I said, fighting back tears.

I reached for her and pulled her in for a hug. I kissed the side of her forehead. I held her longer than normal, lingering so she wouldn't detect my emotions. Once again, I swallowed my tears, quickly pulled it together and released her.

"You're just an early bird and mommy's just a grumpy old gremlin," I joked, saying some stupid shit to get a laugh out of her. She was silly and loved to play.

"You a grumpy gremlin," she snickered.

"Yes, I am," I said with a smile before giving her stomach a light tickle.

She laughed hysterically until I stopped. I kissed her again, this time on one of her chubby cheeks. I held her while I turned her to face me.

"Mommy's going to do better okay."

She nodded. She had no idea how much it took out of me to pretend to be normal.

"Okay," she nodded, assuring her understanding. "Mommy can I have cereal pancake?"

"You sure can."

I chuckled silently and climbed out of bed. I walked Kyllie into the living room and turned on the tv for her while I headed into the bathroom and got myself together. After completing my morning hygiene routine and making sure Kyllie did the same, I headed into the kitchen and made her the pancakes she'd requested.

"Mommy where's Daddy?" Kyllie asked, trailing behind me as I walked her food and cup of milk into the living room.

I thought about pretending not to hear the question but decided not to because I knew that she would just repeat herself.

"I don't know honey," I said truthfully.

"Him might went to grandma's house," she suggested.

"Maybe," I said, sitting her plate and cup down.

Her question lingered in my thoughts. That's where he said he was going, but I knew that he was probably somewhere laid up with Lola. After our argument, I hadn't heard from him. I hadn't bothered to call or text him and he hadn't tried either. I argued but my pride wouldn't allow me to chase behind him and blow up his phone. I'd never been that girl.

Before Kyllie could ask me another question, I was saved by the bell. My phone rang loudly and vibrated from the kitchen counter. It was now a little after nine, and there weren't too many people that called me that early. My baby sister Wave, and my cousin Miracle. I walked off, grabbing my phone off the counter. Wave's number flashed across the screen. I swiped to answer.

"Hey boo!" she said, greeting me in her usual fashion.

"Hey Wave," I said cheerfully. "What's up?"

My circle got small after my son's death, but my

little sister remained at the forefront of it. We were five years apart, but we were tight.

"Ain't shit. Just callin' yo' ass to see what you and TT's Ky baby was doing. Oh! And I wanted to know what you plan to do for your birthday this weekend?"

Wave was going a mile a minute like she usually did. Naturally hyper, I was convinced she had a touch of ADHD or something.

"Girl, I'm not celebrating this year. There's nothing to celebrate about."

I'd actually completely forgotten about the fact that I was about to turn a milestone age. Thirty.

"You should E," Wave urged. "I completely understand not feeling up to it but you gotta try to live. You're turning thirty. It doesn't have to be a club. Let's get out and do something to just ..."

She paused. I knew that she was trying to choose her words carefully.

"Just breathe a little life into you," she finished.

Breathe life into me? I heard her and apparently, she'd heard me. Losing my son had felt like dying. I'd said it so many times. I felt dead inside, so breathing a little life into me was something that would be nearly impossible to do. But I applauded her high hopes.

"I'm not feeling it," I said softly. "It's just going to be a regular weekend for me. I'll probably take Kyllie to her grandma so I can relax and get a moment to myself. You know how demanding she is."

I glanced over at Kyllie who was sitting in the floor

of the living room, making a mess with the fruity pebble pancakes I'd made her. She was quietly watching tv, but I knew that once she was done, she'd be up in my face trying to talk me to death. I loved my baby, but I didn't feel like that shit seven days a week. Saturday morning cartoons used to be what we did together while Quan slept in, but lately she'd been watching alone.

Wave sighed.

"Girl, she practically lives over there," she said, even though it didn't have shit to do with what we were talking about.

"So?" I said defensively. "It saves me money and she ain't got shit else to do no way."

Zalo's mom Carmen was one of those traditional matriarchs that held the family down. She did all the cleaning, cooking, and tending to the kids. That was their culture. The man handled shit, and the woman stayed at home. It had been her husband until he passed away, and now it was Zalo. His mom didn't want for shit. He took care of her household just like he did ours. Hence the reason we lived in an apartment and not in a mini mansion. Hell, she damn near lived better than me. The least she could do was watch her grandchild.

"Damn E. Why are you all sensitive and shit? I'm just saying, TT baby probably tired of going over there with them Spanish speaking motherfuckers eating enchiladas."

I shook my head at Wave' ignorance.

"And don't try to get off topic," she continued with a chuckle. "You need to do something for your birthday."

I exhaled but didn't say anything, so she continued running her mouth like she always did.

"Come on, E. You can't sleep all the time, work and confine yourself to the house. You can't let that shit win," she said sympathetically.

I knew she was talking about the depression. Even though I bottled up my emotions, my circle always acknowledged what I was going through. They knew. Even when I didn't say it. The line fell silent, so Wave continued.

"Well ... how about we have a girl's night," she suggested, as if the idea had just come to her. "Me, you, Tyra, and whoever else you want there."

The idea wasn't bad. I didn't mind a night with a few bitches I loved. They brought me a tiny bit of peace in my sad ass world. I didn't mind a little more of that. Whether they knew it or not, they felt a little like therapy.

"I'll think about it," I told her.

"Yeah, well think about it quick bitch, before I change my mind and be bent over somewhere."

"Eww TMI," I said in disgust.

Although we were five years apart, I felt like I'd raised Wave. I didn't want to hear shit about her rolling around with a nigga.

"Girl please. Don't act like you don't get down!" she laughed. "I done heard about you. Freak ass. That's the reason why Zalo scooped you up so fast and sat that ass down," she cackled.

"Bitch you ain't heard shit," I laughed.

"Mmm-hhm. Keep thinking that."

We both laughed because she and I both knew that I definitely had the niggas. After giving birth, my body snapped right back, only this time my curves had increased by three. My ass was wide and juicy, and I had titties and hips for days. Many would even consider me borderline plus size. I hadn't had to start shopping in those big ass sizes yet, but I was hanging off the cliff at an XL.

"Well listen, I gotta go but I've been meaning to ask, have you talked to Ma lately?" she asked.

"A few days ago. I went by there to make sure she didn't have nobody trying to move the fuck in."

"I know that's right. She might smoke crack, but the house doesn't have to be a crack house," Wave said with a laugh.

"You know what … I'm hanging up. I love you, bye."

I hung up the phone before Wave could say anything else. At twenty-five years old, the girl was crazy and would say anything that came to mind. Our mom in fact did smoke crack from time to time but she wasn't a certified fiend. Liquor was her first love but somehow along the way, she started dabbling in hard drugs. Growing up she kept a lot of people around the house that played cards with her and shared bottles with her. I guess they'd eventually passed the pipe too. And like a damn fool, she took it.

Luckily, for my mom, my grandmother's hard work ensured she'd always have a place to stay. Years ago, she'd purchased a home and left it to my mom and her siblings when she died. My mom had two older brothers neither of them wanted it. I'd been doing repairs here and there to make it better but hadn't really given it any attention in the past year. I decided that I would make it a priority, just in case I needed to go back there.

KYSON MCCARTER

"*I* don't think that's a good idea."

I took a deep breath and bit down on my bottom lip before pausing. Anytime I was about to blow a fuse, it always helped to count to five. *One. Two. Three. Four. Five*. I took a deep breath and thought carefully before replying.

"I don't remember asking, nor do I give a fuck what you think. I haven't seen my fuckin' daughter in a week. I'm picking her up, so you better have her ready, and if you play that not trying to answer the door shit, I'll kick it off the fuckin' hinges," I threatened.

Silence. That's when I realized she'd hung up on me.

"Fuckin' goofy bitch," I muttered.

I clicked the side of my phone and blacked my screen before tossing it onto the kitchen counter. Chelsea knew I wasn't playing, and I'd bet my last dollar that she'd have my daughter ready to go when I got there. She was notorious for trying her hand with me, but I always shut that shit down. I met her six years back after some time in prison. I was twenty-eight years old and after a decade long prison bid, a nigga didn't know any better. Chelsea was one of the first bodies I'd jumped on and I regretted that shit 'til that day. Selfish, entitled, ungrateful. She was the last person I wanted to raise my daughter; yet that's how the cards had been dealt and I was dealing with it.

Still seated at a barstool at the island in the state-of-the-art kitchen, I caught a glimpse of my aunt Kim. She was standing at the sink loading dishes into the dishwasher. My eyes landed and remained fixed on the back of her head. With the water running steadily from the faucet and splashing into the stainless-steel sink, she stood there quietly rinsing dishes and stacking them in the racks of the dishwasher. Her silence was annoying. I knew there was a lot she wanted to say. She *always* had something to say.

Next to my brother Kobra and my daughter Zoe, my auntie was one of the closest people to me. She raised me. She'd always been that hands on auntie, helping out, but she stepped in all the way, when my mom was killed, and my pop was sent to prison for eternity. They hadn't actually given the nigga eternity, but eighty years was practically the same. My pops prison sentence had actually come first, but either way, she'd held us down.

Black with chestnut colored skin, Aunt Kim was a regal woman. Although beautiful, she had been shaped and hardened by the cold streets of West Baltimore. To put it simply, she was no ordinary woman. She had a mouth like a semi-automatic but a heart of gold. She never liked Chelsea and had made that shit clearer than a motherfucker from the beginning. Being able to say, "I told you so," didn't give her satisfaction, it actually pissed her off. She loved my daughter like she was her own grandchild, and she didn't have the patience, nor time, to deal with Chelsea's quarterly shenanigans.

"I know you wanna say something," I finally said, ending the silence in the kitchen. "Say what you gotta say. You came in here to listen to my conversation anyway," I said slightly annoyed.

Between breakfast and lunch, Aunt Kim would usually kick her feet up in the same spot of the gigantic sectional in the living room and watch tv until about eleven thirty. A little before twelve, she'd load dishes and start preparing lunch. Today however, she'd switched her routine to be nosey.

She was a half hour early loading dishes and it was only because she heard me on the phone. I hadn't been just talking to Chelsea. She'd been eavesdropping on my business calls before that.

My Aunt wasn't completely in the game. Because she was a woman, she had one foot in and one foot out. The way it was supposed to go, I ran shit with Kobra's assistance. However, I went to jail as a kid and came out damn near thirty. A nigga was still learning so my auntie ran shit behind the scenes as needed.

After hearing my remark, Aunt Kim turned around slowly and glared at me through questioning eyes. She didn't even have to ask 'who the hell you think you talking to' because her eyeballs acted as her lips.

"Kyson, please don't get the shit slapped out of you first thing this Saturday morning. You're in my house," she reminded me.

I stared her down but remained silent and sat in my thoughts. She knew what I wanted to do but I wouldn't dare say it out of love and respect for my aunt.

"I don't' give a damn who bought it," she said, stealing my thoughts. "It's mine, and you don't get no privacy when you here," she snapped before rolling her eyes and twisting her head back to the sink. "And for you to even request it is crazy as hell."

My jaws tightened as I listened. I knew she wasn't done.

"I told you how that girl was gon' be when you first started rolling around with her."

"I'm not trying to hear that Auntie," I groaned.

"Well just like you told her ... I don't remember asking, nor do I give a fuck," she spat, turning around. "And that's the last time I want to hear you going back and forth with that retarded ass bitch. Go get my niece and right after, make it a priority to get full custody. Ain't no way anyone like her needing to be raising nobody else. You got that?" she asked.

Aunt Kim was as sweet as strawberry icing but when she checked a nigga, she cut down to the bone. She was the only person that could talk to me like a bitch and get away with it. I didn't even play with my pops like that. But with Aunt Kim, it was the other way around: she didn't play with me. Of course, because of who I was, it only took place in privacy. The only other person that had heard her check a nigga like that was my twin brother Kobra, and he got the same treatment.

"Yes ma'am," I mumbled.

"Good," she said before going back to her business.

~

I turned off Governor Ritchie Highway onto Marley Neck Boulevard and after driving for a few miles, I entered the upscale townhouse that my daughter lived in with her mother, Chelsea. Originally from the city, I'd moved the hoe out to Glen Burnie right before Zoe was born. The city of Baltimore was a place that I wanted my baby girl to know nothing of. Two steps ahead, I paid cash for the house because life was short, and I wanted to make sure that my kid had a roof over her head forever. I also knew that my baby mama wasn't used to shit and irresponsible. If something happened to me, her money-hungry ass would probably try to sell that motherfucker before my body was cold in the ground, so when I purchased the house, I'd put it in my name and Zoe's name with the intention of it becoming hers completely when she became legal age.

Like the simple bitch she was, Chelsea had never inquired about any documentation. I'd shown her a receipt for the purchase and that was good enough for her. Never once did she inquire about the deed. I knew then that her ass wasn't the brightest star in the sky.

Chelsea had played in my face the first few months I dealt with her by pretending to be decent. By the time I realized that she was a bad doing, no money and no motion having bitch, she was months pregnant with my seed. From that moment, I knew I would be taking care of both her and my daughter for many years to come.

The crib was the first task. My second task was putting her in a new whip to drive my daughter around. I didn't get any fancy shit. Her ass had a brand-new van delivered to her front step that she refused to drive.

Parked a few houses down on the side of the street, I admired Chelsea's multi-colored house, along with the other homes in the community. I'd picked it out myself. Three story, modern, and in an upscale, resort-like community, I'd paid nearly half million for it. It wasn't no shit like what my auntie had, but it was comfortable enough for my daughter when she wasn't with me. The goal was that she was with me more often than not. Lately, Chelsea had been trying to play games with me coming and going for my daughter like I'd usually been. Taking days to answer her phone and not being home when I came by. Why? I wasn't sure. But time always revealed everything.

I brought my wrist up and glanced at the time on my stainless-steel Audemar. A little over an hour had passed since Chelsea had hung the phone up on me. I was still low-key irritated about that. Her doing that slick shit and then Aunt Kim talking shit had put me in a dangerous mood.

I had already parked so I killed the engine of my Lamborghini Urus. Despite it being broad daylight, I still scanned the neighborhood from the tinted interior. A nigga like me always had to be on point to avoid getting caught slipping. After confirming that I hadn't been followed or there were no niggas lurking, I jumped out and made my way towards the house. I brushed the invisible lint off my lay as I proceeded to glide across the street to my destination.

"How you doing?" I greeted the white middle-aged woman with a smile and a wave.

She'd just walked out of her door towards her car and appeared to be headed to work, judging by the pantsuit she wore.

"Hi Kyson!" she said chipperly, showing a row of straight white teeth. "I'm pretty good. How about yourself?" she asked.

"Not too bad," I replied. "Good seeing you," I replied, keeping it short.

"You too," she said, opening the door of her Lexus and hopping in.

Sarah, the neighbor had moved in right before Chelsea did. Initially, I was around a lot until my relationship with Chelsea had completely ended. Up until that time, I'd built a rapport with several of the neighbors. Sarah and her husband Scott, more so. My daughter, Zoe, played with their kids and a few times, they'd even had us over for dinner.

Sarah's car roared to life as I walked up the front steps. When I got to the door, I brought my keys up to unlock it but then remembered Chelsea had them changed. I pushed my keys into my pocket and knocked firmly.

After about ten seconds of waiting, I knocked again. Only this time, harder. I didn't have a lot of patience, so I wasn't big on waiting.

"I'm coming!"

Chelsea's voice sounded from inside. After a bit of shuffling, she swung the door open, looking just as irritated as I was. Face to face, I couldn't help but take in her appearance. Despite the annoyed look she wore, she was undeniably beautiful. Brown skin. Angelic features. Short pixie cut hair that she kept an auburn color. She was naturally gorgeous, and her looks were the reason why she felt entitled to everything, while contributing absolutely fucking nothing.

"Move," I demanded, pushing past her petite frame to get inside. I walked ahead of her towards the kitchen,

"Nigga don't be waltzing all up in my house like you pay some damn bills," she said sharply.

"You'd like that wouldn't you, unfortunately, yo' pussy doesn't command all the extras. The only reason you got this, is because of my daughter," I reminded her. "You should be thankful."

I turned around and smiled at her while her face transformed to anger.

"Fuck you Kyson. Wait here. She's getting ready."

"I figured she would be," I said calmly.

I watched Chelsea's back as she walked off down the hall and into my daughter's room, returning shortly after. I had no real issues with my baby mom except she was entitled and selfish. Oh, and a whore too. I should had known her character was questionable when she fucked and sucked me dry the very first day that I'd met her. The pussy and mouth were decent, so I kept her around. For some reason, the bean-head bitch thought I was foolish enough to wife her up. I was a player. I changed bitches like I changed my drawers. A female that showed zero of the qualities I was looking for in the long run, would never be my girl. She'd fooled herself thinking that she could fake those qualities. When it became crystal clear that I was no sucka, she trapped me.

It was crazy how at my peak I was fucking four or five bitches on the regular, but the only one that wound up pregnant was the one that was talking about being an official couple. Chelsea.

After getting one of those prenatal DNA tests, it was confirmed I was the daddy. Although she was the last bitch I wanted a kid by, I was kind of happy. A nigga had never created shit. Of course, Chelsea was glad too, thinking that a baby would solidify a relationship. She was wrong of course, and she'd been bitter ever since.

While I waited by the door, as Chelsea had requested, she walked into the living room and took a seat on the couch. Her little ass jiggled with every step in the silk nightgown she wore. I openly admired her and even thought about spreading that ass apart and running up in that warm pussy a few more times. Then I quickly remembered how much of a headache she was when I was sticking dick in her.

"Zoe! Hurry up, your dad's out here waiting!" Chelsea yelled from the living room about a minute later when she hadn't emerged yet.

"Okay!" I heard my daughter's sweet voice call back.

Hearing it made me smile. It was a reminder that despite all the bad things I'd done, I had some good attached to me.

"She's five," I reminded Chelsea, cutting my eyes at her where she was sitting. "It would help if you got off yo' ass and go help her."

I looked at her and waited for a response; however, she chose to ignore me. She instead continued sitting on the couch Indian-style, watching some bullshit on tv, instead of helping my daughter with her bags. I didn't understand why she didn't have that shit packed and ready in the living room when she knew I was coming. I wasn't one of those lying ass dads. If I said I was pulling up, I was pulling up. I shook my head, but suddenly felt the weight of urine on my bladder. I began walking to the bathroom to relieve myself since I was waiting anyway.

"Where the fuck you going?" Chelsea asked as I

began walking from the door towards the back of the house where the bathroom was located.

Her eyes had flickered when she saw me moving. Like it had made her instantly nervous. Any other time she didn't seem to mind me walking all through the crib. I was very good at reading body language and hers was a no-brainer. She had a nigga in the crib.

"You got a nigga in here?" I asked, pausing my footsteps.

My eyes darkened while I waited for a response. I didn't like playing games, nor beating around the bush. My temper was murderous, and shit could go from zero to homicide very quickly. My aunt and father stayed on me about that shit. *"How the fuck can you be a boss when you move off emotions?"* It was some shit I was still working on.

"Hell no! And if I did, it's none of your business," she quickly replied.

Her mouth said one thing, but her eyes said another. I didn't believe her. Like I said before, I could read motherfuckers very well. Her entire body language had changed, and she was no longer sitting Indian style. She had one leg underneath her, but her other foot was now planted on the floor like she was ready to take off into a full sprint.

"It would be my business because one, you have my daughter in here, and two, I bought this house for her. You want to lay up with a nigga, go to his crib."

I was ready to go in on her, but she cut me off.

"Zoe! Hurry up, your dad's *leaving*," she said as if she had the power to put me out.

It was something about the way she kept trying me, that set me off. Without saying another word, I stormed to the back of the crib, but I was no longer heading to the bathroom. I was headed to her room to verify what I already knew.

"Kyson!" she called out, running behind me. "Kyson! Don't go in my room!" she yelled, pulling on my shirt.

The bitch had sprinted towards me like she was loss prevention at Macy's. Like a nigga was stealing or something.

"Get the fuck back," I growled, pushing her a little harder than I intended.

"Daddy?" I heard my daughter's voice call, but that wasn't enough to stop me.

She emerged at the entrance of her doorway just as I was storming past.

"Get her," I said to Chelsea before either of them could follow me.

All that noise Chelsea had made had alerted my daughter to the fact that some shit was about to go down.

"Zoe honey go back into your room and close the door. Don't come out until I say so," Chelsea said with panic in her voice.

Her actions and tone confirmed what I knew. The bitch's audacity intensified my anger. I didn't care about Chelsea dating. She could fuck and suck on a dog's dick for all I cared. It was the fact that this was my daughter's home. It wasn't for her to be laid up butt-naked with a nigga. It was for her to raise my little girl in a safe and stable environment.

As soon as I got to Chelsea's bedroom, I turned the knob and pushed open the door. My eyes immediately landed on a dark-skinned nigga. He was laid up in the bed, stretched out, watching tv, shirtless with boxers on. Hearing me enter, his expression changed from peaceful to confused. His brows dipped, but before he could ask any questions, or introduce himself, I charged him. Snatching him out of the bed by his arm, I pulled him to the floor where he landed with a hard thud.

"Yo, what the fuck?" he asked, through quarter sized eyes.

His arms were extended out, as if ready to beg for mercy. He was a young nigga. Late twenties with a slim but fit build, and shoulder-length dreads. I did a quick scan of the room to locate any guns. I knew Chelsea didn't own one but a nigga like him, probably had one close by. I didn't see one.

"Shut up nigga!" I spat before cocking my arm back and punching him in the face so hard, both his lips split open.

That one hit had blood spewing from his mouth like someone had turned on a faucet. I wasn't satisfied though. I had a point to prove. I hit him again. The second punch landed in the middle of his face. I heard a few bones crunch. I'd probably broke his nose. He'd be sporting two black eyes soon and that temporarily satisfied me. I slowed down my assault and allowed him to speak.

"Yo, please man! What the fuck!" he begged.

Blood seeped from his mouth as he talked and one of his front teeth was gone.

"Shut yo' bitch ass up," I said with a hard kick to his side.

He groaned in pain, spitting out the tooth he'd lost in the process.

"Apparently, this bitch didn't tell you that you in a crib that I paid for and since she wanna disrespect my motherfucking child, I gotta disrespect you!" I growled, standing over top of him.

I didn't hit women so my only way to deal with Chelsea was to hit her differently. Her stupid ass was worried about bouncing and sucking on dick, but once I was done with this one, he'd never want to fuck with her again. Like I said before, I didn't care what she did, as long as she kept it away from my daughter. I was a mean, petty, and spiteful nigga. I'd paid for that crib and for her to think that she could fuck and suck on my dime had me livid. The bitch barely wanted to pay to keep the lights on. I gave her money every month to make sure the utilities were paid, and my daughter had food. I funded her fucking life. I felt disrespected and I wanted to break her neck. But I couldn't, so he would settle for now.

"Get the fuck off of him!" Chelsea demanded, running into the room.

"Or what?" I said, standing up swiftly with a grin.

I eyed her menacingly, but she said nothing. She instead stopped in her tracks.

"Like I thought," I spat.

I leaned back down, pushed my hand against his throat and began squeezing..

"Ahhhhhh," he gagged, immediately trying to fight for air.

His hands now clung to mine, scratching and clawing desperately for me to release him.

"Shut the fuck up," I growled while squeezing tighter. "Don't let this bitch get you killed in here little nigga. I promise you, she ain't worth it."

"Stop Kyson. Please stop," Chelsea begged. "You're going to fucking kill him," she argued while doing her best to keep her voice down.

"Maybe," I threatened, squeezing even tighter.

I was squeezing so hard my fingers ached. Green veins appeared on his face. His brown complexion was turning red. He continued clawing weakly at my grip. He didn't stand a chance. If I wanted him dead, then that's what he would be.

Chelsea was now standing on the side of me pulling at my arms, but it wasn't enough. I wouldn't look at her or budge. My eyes were locked with his. Watching as life began to slowly slip away from him.

"I could kill him," I taunted, without looking up at her. "Break his neck … Or even strangle him to death. It's that fuckin easy."

His eyes started to flutter, and his body began to

show defeat. He was no longer fighting. His gasps for air had become pants.

"Please Kyson! Please! Stop!" she yelled out.

This time, she didn't care about how loud she was. Her pleas were urgent because she knew that time was winding down.

"I don't give a fuck if you sell yo' tired ass pussy to the highest bidder, just don't do it in this house or while my daughter is with you."

"Okay Kyson! Okay! Just please. Let him go! Zoe is in the other room. Don't do this."

Zoe ... The mention of my daughter's name broke me out of my trance. I could've killed him, but I wouldn't. What kind of father would I be if I killed a man while she stood in the next room? I'd surely go to jail because Chelsea would tell the police who'd done it. And then, all the cameras. I looked up at Chelsea and gave her a look that one reserved for their greatest enemies. My anger had surfaced from pride. I simply hated when motherfuckers tried to play with me. My name rang bells through the city of Baltimore. I was respected and I'd worked hard to earn it. I wasn't sure if the nigga knew who I was, but I still felt disrespected. But it wasn't his fault. It was Chelsea's fault. I'd let her get away with shit so long that she'd begun disrespecting me without thinking, and in a sense, had other people doing it with her. I'd made my point with him. It was time for me to *really* make my point with her. I released his neck.

While he lay on the floor, gasping and thankful for

another shot at life, I got right up in Chelsea's face and mushed her in the center of her forehead.

"This your first, and final warning," I said to her in a near whisper. "Zoe's coming with me and when you get yo' shit together, maybe she can come visit."

"You're not taking my daughter nowhere," Chelsea said, still trying to employ her imaginary power.

I took a deep breath. *One, two, three, four, five.* I counted in my head. My fists clenched at the sides. I wanted to beat her ass so bad. Just one punch was all. One punch to her fucking face would make me feel better. I couldn't do it because I knew that one punch would cause her to sail across the fucking room. But God, how I wanted to step outside of my character for just one second.

"Watch me," I said in response.

I looked down at the pathetic ass nigga still laying on the floor one final time and then headed out the room.

Chelsea didn't try to stop me. I heard her drop to her knees and began consoling the nigga I'd just beat on. She already knew that I was taking my daughter whether she liked it or not.

EASTON BLUE

"*E*aston! Easton!"

I blinked a few times and looked to my left where my best friend Tyra stood, calling me repeatedly. Her toffee-colored face was etched with worry.

"Huh?" I finally replied.

"You okay?"

I nodded a quick yes. I had gotten lost in my thoughts, thinking about how life was when it was perfect. When it was all four of us. Remembering back to when Quan had passed the test for his driver's license. How he'd jumped up and down for joy at the accomplishment, because despite going to the best driving school in the city, he'd failed twice because of his inability to parallel park. He'd been so excited. Even more thrilled when Zalo handed him the keys to his first car: a GLA 250. The vehicle he would die in.

I looked down at one of the butt-length braids I was plaiting. I zoned out a lot while I worked. Doing hair was like therapy and rightfully, I became very relaxed and got lost in my thoughts while doing so. Of course, Tyra had her reasons for asking that question. *You okay?* I didn't feel some type of way. I felt a lot of ways, but I kept them nestled deep inside of me. Tyra had been my rock for so long and I didn't want to put any more on her. I wanted to give her a break.

"I'm fine."

I forced a reassuring smile and then diverted my gaze back to the braid in my hand. I carefully reexamined it for imperfections. There were none. There never were. I was good at what I did. Actually, I was excellent. In fact, I was one of the best braiders in B-More. Wasn't nobody fucking with me on the braid tip. Knotless, boho, mermaid braids, island twists. I had that shit on lock. Even better than the Africans. Minus the bald ass edges them bitches often left you with.

I'd been braiding hair since I was thirteen, my skills aging like fine wine. I was well aware of my talent, so my prices were high, and I refused to budge on them.

"Okay. Well, you think you can take another head?" Tyra asked. "It's a kid though," she warned.

I stopped working on the extra small knotless I was doing and turned my head to the side to face her. She already knew the answer to that question.

"A kid? Hell naw."

I couldn't stand doing kids hair. They cried, complained and they never sat their ass still. I spent more time twisting and turning on their heads than actually braiding. They also never got anything significant or worth my damn time. On adults, I could charge $450 for some extra small knotless and up to $600 for small boho knotless with human hair. Most of the time, parents didn't want to pay for much except for some big braids or a head full of natural plaits with beads. $75 and $100 jobs.

The shop we worked was called The Hair Bistro. It was busy and to do Tyra that favor, there was a possibility that I could miss a walk-in that wanted a service that was double or triple than what I would be getting for a child's head. I didn't feel like dealing with some booger-nose brat that I'd want to pinch and push when her parent wasn't looking.

"Come on E. Do it for me. Her father made her an appointment a week ago and I overbooked myself. He paid in full already. Please," she begged.

I huffed and rolled my eyes at Tyra.

"T, I'm not trying to be tied up on no kids head missing *real* money," I argued. "Call and get one of those other hoes to do it. They need the money more than I do," I said.

There were a few other girls in the shop that we worked with, but they worked sporadically, and the only ones that were consistent were me and Tyra. We were the most popular stylists, and everyone requested us. Me for braids and Tyra for braids *and* installs. The lady that owned the suite never came in, so we practically ran the place.

"Girl please. Them hoes aren't consistent. You see it's Saturday and we're the only two working."

She cocked her head and pursed her lips to help prove her point.

"Those bitches don't want no money for real, *and* none of them are *you*. Plus, the client doesn't come 'til six-fifteen. You have now, until closing time, so you won't be missing anything." She sighed, clearly desperate. "They're the last appointment and you never do any styles that won't have you done by six-thirty. As fast as you are, her hair will be done in thirty, forty minutes," she argued.

She was right. Tyra knew me almost as well as I knew myself. The days I worked, I started at ten in the morning, and I'd usually get my last customer out of the chair by six-thirty, that way I could be out by seven. If I took Tyra's kiddie client, I could have her in and out of my chair by seven. It would keep me in the shop a little later, but essentially, it would be putting a little extra money in my pocket.

"Why the hell can't you do it?" I quizzed.

"Because I had a last-minute appointment that came in a few minutes ago for a full sew-in with a lace closure. Hair included. She's coming in at five-thirty. It's gonna push me into the little girl's appointment and I can't have her waiting that long."

I sighed but now completely understood her logic. That one, last-minute appointment would get her an easy $650. Tyra was my bitch so one thing I wasn't about to do was keep her from getting some money. Being overbooked and having people waiting was unprofessional as fuck and there was no way she could stop that sew-in and do a child's head. For the type of money homegirl was spending, the service she received should be top tier.

"So, you got me?" she asked, after a minute or so passed by.

I looked back at her, and she had her lip poked out in a pout.

"Girl, I don't care about you pouting," I laughed. "Yeah, I got you, but if her little ass get in here showing off, you owe me dinner."

"I gotchu boo," Tyra said, before clapping her hands in relief.

After braiding for a few more hours, I was done with the extra small knotless I had been working on. I held a pile of them in my hand, digging through them and moving them from side to side. They looked good, and my client was happy. I could tell by the way she was moving her head and grinning all up in the mirror that I had handed to her.

"So, we're almost done. I've already put the kettle on the stove," I assured my client, since she'd already mentioned twice that she was running behind schedule. We'd gotten a little behind because of bathroom breaks and one food break.

"Okay," she said, handing the mirror back for me to put up.

While I waited for the water to boil nearby, I went up and down her braids, snipping any strands sticking off. A few minutes later, the timer began beeping, signaling that the water was heated to the appropriate temperature.

"I'm gonna dip you and then mousse you down. After that, you'll be ready to go."

With my stylist cape tied tightly around me, I walked off to where I had my dipping kettle plugged in. A few seconds later, I heard heavy shuffling and then my best friend's voice.

"Ay yo! What the fuck!" I heard Tyra yell, causing me to spin around.

The hoe had jumped up out of the chair and bolted to the door.

"Bitch! I know the fuck not!" I yelled, quickly putting the kettle down and running behind her.

She snatched open the door, the chime of the bell sounding through the shop. That's when that bitch became Usain Bolt. Before I had even reached the door, her ass had taken off full speed like an Olympic gold medalist down the block. I thought about running after her but my acrylic toes in a pair of Chanel slides had me rethink that. It was unlikely that I'd catch her and I wouldn't do shit but wind up busting my ass.

"Bum ass bitch!" I yelled, my professionalism going out the door.

I screamed a few more obscenities out of frustration and then looked at Tyra's client.

"I'm sorry ma'am," I said half-heartedly.

"No, you're okay honey. You have every right to be upset. She wrong for that," the woman in Tyra's chair said, shaking her head.

Four hundred and fifty dollars had literally just run through the door. Hours of hard work. All for nothing.

"Ima beat that bitch's ass if I ever catch her," I said, punching the palm of my hand. "Baltimore's small so somebody knows her."

I plopped down angrily into the chair that I serviced my clients. I was so mad, I could've cried. It wasn't just about the money. It was the fact that bitches were bums, and I had worked on her broke-ass head for hours. I hated feeling like a bitch got one up on me.

"Call the police," Tyra suggested. "That's theft of services. Don't you have your clients upload their license when they book?"

Of course, the answer to that question was no. I exhaled a frustrated breath. I wasn't irritated with Tyra. More at the situation.

"No girl. But I got her IG handle."

I scurried over to my purse to get my phone. I went straight to Instagram to look her up, but the bitch already had me blocked. The hoe was already one step ahead of me. I sucked my teeth and shook my head at the fuckery.

"This bum bitch already blocked me. She probably blocked me before she even got here. Probably never had any intention of paying. Look her up T. Her name is coldred410."

"I'm blocked too," Tyra said, already on it.

"I can look her up for y'all," Tyra's client said.

"Please, I would really appreciate it."

"Yeah, no problem. I can't stand that kind of bullshit. Y'all work too hard for y'all money," she argued. "You said coldred410?"

"Yeah."

After pulling out her phone and typing for a little, she brought her phone up for me to examine.

"This her?" she asked.

I took the phone, eyed the profile picture on the screen and sure enough, it was her.

"Can you screenshot that and send it to me. That hoe wanna run out on me, I'm about to embarrass her broke ass."

"Fuck!" I yelled out randomly, letting what just happen sink in. "Half of my days' pay."

I'd done a set of medium knotless when I first arrived at ten, but I'd only charged $300 for those. From one to six, I'd stood over top of that hoe head. I was expecting to take home $750 for the day but was leaving with less than half that.

I didn't do hair because I needed the money. Zalo had money, but it was nothing like getting my own. I always had, and I always would.

"Shit like this fucks it up for others. I'm requiring full payment from now on. Unless they're a regular and I know for sure they good, they're paying in full."

I grabbed my phone off my station. I was going right to my booking site and making that change right away. I was doing hoes a favor by even working in the city. I could've gone out to the county, tacked extra on my services and made all the bitches from the city drive all the way out.

"Girl don't stress that shit. You got enough on your plate. I gotchu when I'm done. I'll split with you. You'll still lose a little but not the full amount."

That's why I loved Tyra. Because of her selflessness and her heart. Always looking out for others.

"No girl," I quickly told her.

Tyra had a house full of bills that she paid by herself and I wasn't about to pull from that. I was more than good. I was really just frustrated.

"These hoes are paying in full from now on. All it takes is one time for a bitch to get me. I appreciate you offering but keep yo' money in yo' pocket. You know I'm cool. We got food and I ain't facing eviction," I laughed.

Tyra and I had been friends since high school. She knew my struggle coming up. Even though I did hair, back then, I had no real clientele outside of random people from the hood that I knew or girls from my high school. I made money but not enough. If they weren't choosing to go to someone more skilled than I was, they wouldn't return as quickly as I needed them to. People wore braids for a month or so and then let their hair breathe. My clients weren't running back and forth to me for that reason. It had been plenty of times Tyra gave me the last in her pocket to get Quan shit like Pedialyte or pull ups. Other times, she'd bring me shit she'd stolen. Tyra had been through so many rough times with me. Utility shut off's and no food. If I couldn't make something happen, then my best friend would. There wasn't a bitch like Tyra. Not my sister. Not my cousin. Nobody.

"Okay boo. And I'm sorry that fuck shit happened to you. I hope we're together when you run into that hoe. Stomp the braids and edges out that bitch's head."

Although I was irritated, I couldn't help but laugh. Tyra was and always would be a mess.

Less than fifteen minutes later, a man and a little girl that looked to be five or six, walked through the door. There were only three of us in the shop, but everyone paused when they entered. The girl was adorable in a cute pant set with princesses on them. She was a cute child that could surely light up any room with her fat cheeks and wide eyes. However, her daddy …. Her daddy stole the gotdamn show. The man was fucking gorgeous. I mean, enough to stop a group of bitches while they were talking. I brushed a tendril hanging sloppily from a loose ponytail out of my eye. For a moment, I felt inadequate. I'd walked out of the house prepared to work and had put zero thought into my look.

At first glance, it was clear that the fine ass man that walked in was a hood nigga. Masculine, yet beautiful. Think rapper Dave East, although he didn't look shit like him. This man was his own work of art and there wasn't a soul that could be compared to him. Baltimore had some rough looking people and that wasn't to throw shade. That was just facts. Both women and men. Outside of Zalo, it was rare to see a man that fine. Fit but beefy build. Sun-kissed brown skin, and braids that hung against the side of his face. Full luscious lips. Dark brows. Low mysterious eyes. I couldn't say it enough; the man was fine.

"Y'all gon' say hello? Or you just gon' stare at a nigga on some retarded shit?" he asked, clearly irritated.

That quickly, his looks no longer existed or mattered. He'd become ugly.

"I'm sorry. Are you here for the six-fifteen appointment?" Tyra asked, snapping out of the trance his presence had us all in.

"Yeah," he said. "Six o'clock, six-fifteen, whatever." He shrugged. "I'm just trying to get in and out."

I glanced at the zebra clock on the wall in the black and white color themed shop. It was only twelve minutes after six.

"Okay, well she can go ahead and have a seat right in that chair over there. That's Easton. She's going to be servicing her today."

Tyra put down the tools she was using and walked over to the little girl.

"Cool," he said, choosing not to acknowledge me.

"I'm sorry, what's her name?" Tyra asked, turning back to him. "Your name is Kyson right? That's what the booking's under."

He nodded. It seemed as if his rude demeanor came naturally. As if he was disconnected from everything and everyone.

"Her name's Zoe," he said, still wearing the same annoyed look he had when he opened his mouth.

"Hi Zoe," Tyra said, ignoring Kyson's attitude and leaning down to speak to the little girl directly. "You can go have a seat in Miss Easton's chair. She's going to take good care of you."

Zoe walked over and after a bit of a struggle, I helped her into my chair and hiked it up with my foot to bring her high enough to get started. I examined the large bush on her head. She had a lot of hair. I took her scrunchie out and quickly observed that it was matted in the middle. It looked like someone just brushed the sides to get it into a ponytail instead of actually combing through it. I became instantly annoyed and cursed under my breath before walking off. Apparently, he noticed my irritation.

"The fuck is you annoyed or something?" Kyson asked as I moved around grabbing all the extra shit I needed to tend to his child's nappy ass hair. "Better get that shit together," he said sharply.

I stopped in my tracks, turned around and eyed him with dipped brows and confusion.

"Who you talking to?" I asked him, my eyes narrowing.

I'd already had a long ass day, and I could tell he was about to fuck it up some more. It was funny that he'd come through the door on bullshit and had the nerve to call me out when I had a legit reason to be annoyed.

"You the only one in this mafucka with their face balled up on some negative shit," he said in return.

The nerve of this nigga.

"Fix that shit before you get over top of my daughter head," he demanded like he was King Tut or some shit.

"First of all, don't come in here and keep getting fucking smart. You walked through the door being ignorant and nobody said shit. You didn't even have the decency to acknowledge me when she introduced me as your daughter's stylist. Second of all, her hair is tangled as shit in the middle and looks like it hasn't been combed in fuckin' ages," I snapped.

I was doing my best to really not go off on his ass. He had the wrong bitch on the right day. I was already acting way out of my character by saying what I'd just said. He was about to make me go way off script.

"The service comes with a wash and blow dry not a full detangling service. And she has a head full of hair so it's gonna take God knows how long to untangle this shit," I said, looking down at her head.

I was trying to be professional, but it was over for that. He wanted to come in talking shit, so I was gonna match his raggedy ass energy. That's all they seemed to understand in Baltimore. I didn't like doing that type of shit in front of kids but the way her daddy talked, I was certain she was used to it.

"That's what you get paid for dummy," he quipped. "The sooner you stop running yo' big ass mouth, the sooner you'll be done," he countered, taking a seat in the waiting area near the window.

I bit my bottom lip, took a deep breath and walked

back over to where his daughter was seated quietly. I looked down at her head.

Now, I'd be wrong if I raked through her nappy shit and had her in here crying.

I guess he could read my thoughts because he suddenly glared at me.

"Don't try no stupid shit either. I promise you, it's not worth it," he said with a threatening grin.

I rolled my eyes in response. He might've been scary on the streets, but he was hardly intimidating walking around, holding the hand of a preschooler. I didn't have time to go back and forth with him. I also didn't have time to be coughing and airing out the shop because I maced his stupid ass. It wasn't the first time that I had to mace a motherfucker in there and if he kept carrying on, it wouldn't be the last.

"I'm sorry but can y'all please stop with the back and forth and all the cursing," Tyra said. "Especially not in front of the little girl."

She then faced Kyson from where she was standing and addressed him directly.

"I understand you may have had a bad day or maybe that's just how you are naturally, but please be respectful."

"Respectfully ma'am. Don't nobody check me. I say what I want," he said waving Tyra off. "I paid to get my daughter hair done and I'm not leaving 'til it's done. And I ain't being disrespectful. This just how I talk."

My jaws clenched. This was why I didn't like

helping people. Tyra paused for a second and then excused herself from her client and walked over to me.

"E just get her in and out. The sooner you get her done, the sooner his rude, ignorant ass can get the fuck out," she whispered into my ear.

I wanted to protest. Rude motherfuckers like him and broke motherfuckers like the bitch that just ran out were the reason why I continuously second guessed my decision to work in the city. Little did Tyra know, but I was about to relocate and take my services elsewhere. She could keep this hood shit.

I didn't even bother replying. I just nodded. Tyra walked off and I knelt down and began talking to the little girl. I could tell she was used to her daddy's bull-shit because she didn't seem the least bit fazed by it.

"Hi sweetheart. I'm sorry you heard us going back and forth. I see a princess on your shirt. Do you like princesses?"

"Yeah," she answered.

"Well, I'm gonna get you taken care of, so you can leave out looking just like the princesses you love so much."

I smiled and gently rubbed her back before standing back up.

"So, your daddy booked you for individuals. Did you want beads or barrettes?

"She getting beads," Kyson cut in from the waiting room.

I wanted to tell him to shut the fuck up and mind his fucking business, but I remembered she actually

52

was his business. He was her father, he was paying, and he ultimately had the final say so. I frowned but didn't allow my intrusive thoughts to win.

"Beads it is," I said directly to her, ignoring her father.

I threw a cape on her and then took her to the wash bowl. I figured it would be easier to detangle her hair wet, rather than dry. I was right, because after a few good shampoos and a condition, I was able to separate her hair into sections and detangle it with ease. Her hair actually wasn't nappy at all. Just neglected.

About an hour and a half later, I had baby girl's hair clean, blow dried and braided up with a bunch of noisy beads at the end. It was too cute, and I could tell she loved it by the way she showed all her teeth in the mirror I'd handed her. I was thankful that she was leaving happy, especially since a forty-five-minute style had taken ninety.

"You like it?" I asked her.

"Yeah," she said softly.

She was on the shy side, but she was actually one of the best child clients I'd ever done.

"Well, you are all done. You did a great job today and you can come back whenever you need your hair done again. Ask for Easton."

I unsnapped her cape and then knelt down so I could whisper something to her.

"Just don't bring your daddy," I told her.

She giggled as I stood back to my feet.

"Fuck you say to her?" he asked, walking over to us with a sly grin.

"I told her she did a good job and that she's done."

I sashayed off before he could respond. I was ready to go home, and so was Tyra. She was sitting at the receptionist's desk waiting for me to finish. After the day that I'd had and the way he'd come in there acting, I had no desire to indulge in any type of chit chat.

"Damn. You must not want yo' tip?" Kyson said, standing there eyeing me in what appeared to be a bit of disbelief.

I guessed he was used to folks waiting on rewards after his approval. I never expected his rude ass to tip, but when I saw him dig in his pocket and pull out a bankroll, I changed my tune.

"Actually, I do," I said, turning around and going back to him with my hand out.

He quickly peeled from the knot he held and shoved two $100 bills in my hand. I figured he went heavy on the tip because of how big of an asshole he'd been. If I was a poor hoe, my eyes would have widened but instead, I just murmured a 'thank you'. He was lucky he even got that.

"Yo' attitude bad as a motherfucker but you got my baby girl right and she's happy, so I appreciate your services," he said.

Despite being surprised, I didn't reply. I just rolled my eyes as he grabbed his daughter's hand and carried his ass out the door.

"Bitch you owe me more than dinner," I told Tyra,

going behind the receptionist desk where she was sitting and grabbing my purse.

She shook her head and stood up while I grabbed my things and stuffed the $100 bill into my pocket.

"You might have to toot that ass up or something," I joked, slapping Tyra on her fat butt.

"Bitch, don't play."

Tyra swatted my hand away from her ass before we burst into laughter and headed out the door so we could lock up.

EGYPT TESTAYE

*H*ow the fuck did I get myself into this shit? Staring up at the ceiling for the past five minutes, the reality of my life had hit me all of a sudden. And hard. All the questions that I should have been asked myself now seemed to invade my thoughts.

How did I let this nigga try to lock me down like this? I sighed deeply. *And why the fuck had I let the games go on so long?*

Greed had led me to get caught up, and what had started off as a game was no longer that. It was real life with people's real feelings involved. It had to end and as scary as it was, I knew I was the one that was going to have to end it. I knew how Benny felt about me, but his time was up. I just hoped he allowed things to end peacefully.

Lying across my California king-size bed, I lay naked with a sheet draped loosely over my body, listening to the steady stream of water tap against the polished marble shower floor in the bathroom. The shower was where Benny stood washing away my scent and all traces of me.

He'd just fucked me up and down my bedroom. Like I belonged to him. Leaving his semen inside of me to grow. Only there was no room because something or should I say, someone was already growing inside of me. He just hadn't been informed. He never would be. In the beginning, I thought about telling him, but then I remembered that he was married. My baby would come into the world being automatically placed beneath a man's wife. That's right, *his wife*.

I knew Benny was married before he even stepped to me in his size 12's. I always did my homework and was a firm believer in *"Can't no nigga play you unless you let him."* I knew I wanted him before Benny even knew he wanted me. Before he knew I existed. I was a hoe. A pretty ass hoe at that. What I saw, I got, and what I got, I conquered. Benny was no exception. Only Benny was no ordinary man. He was a Lieutenant in the infamous, Baltimore Money Mob. A leader in a gang of niggas who slung drugs, ran the city, and killed people. He'd looked me dead in my eyes and told me his feelings weren't to be played with. I was to act accordingly or there would be consequences. With dollar signs in my eyes, I agreed, and now I was about to find out if all the shit he'd said was bluff. I'd spotted a bigger fish, and I was ready to try and catch it. Benny was now, just in my way.

While in thought, Benny walked out of the bathroom with his towel half-way wrapped around his large, damp form. A haze of steam followed him. His eyes fell on my body. Admiration glimmered in his eyes. He knew I was the shit just like I knew it. Petite and chocolate, with angelic features, I was a timeless beauty. No makeup needed. Minimal effort required.

"You leaving?" I asked, pretending to be disappointed.

I allowed my mouth to fall into a pout to make it believable. I was a master at this shit and that's why I was at the top of the hoe game. Benny didn't answer my question right away.

"I got to. We already talked about this shit," he said in his deep voice.

"I know baby. I'm just sad is all. I'm not tripping or trying to stress you," I assured him, doing my best to gently stroke his ego.

Niggas thrived off that shit. They wanted to feel desired and important. There wasn't a soul around that could convince Benny that he wasn't my king. Despite being married, Benny had made it clear that I was his bitch. Initially I didn't welcome the title, especially because Benny was respected and if I wanted to fuck with another boss in the same city in the future, it was likely that they'd run amongst the same circle or had done business together. Benny had me by his side for the long haul and the fact was, I was simply passing through.

I rose up from where I was laying and got on my knees. After crawling to the edge of the bed where

Benny sat, now naked, I wrapped my arms around his back and kissed the side of his face. My fingers trailed the outline of the tattoo on the right side of his chest. A slug. He was deep in thought. It was something that he always did after a shower. Sat on the edge of the bed and just thought. Every now and then, I'd ask him what was on his mind, even though I didn't give a damn.

"I hope you have more time this weekend and didn't forget my birthday is Friday," I said, with another gentle kiss, this one on the side of his lips.

"Ya birthday?" he asked, now pulled from his thoughts. He turned his head to the side to see my face.

"Yeah," I giggled. "I've been reminding you."

He fell silent and I knew why. His anniversary with his wife was the weekend. That was the reason I picked Friday for my birthday. It wasn't my real birthday of course. Just a made-up day so I had a reason to become angry with him. I knew Benny wasn't going to tell me his weekend was already full. He was going to either try to get me to celebrate early or make up an excuse for why he was missing in action. Like I said before, I'd done my research. Benny and his wife's actual anniversary was Thursday and from what I saw, they usually went out of town and celebrated multiple days. She was his priority that weekend.

I was always ahead of the game. I did my research, I snooped, and I knew people that knew them. I was making my exit soon and there wasn't shit he could do about it.

EASTON BLUE

*T*hirty. A milestone age that didn't mean a damn thing to me even though it should have.

The day was October 5th. My thirtieth birthday. The official day that I transitioned from a decade in my twenties to the dirty thirties. It was usually celebrated elaborately but that wasn't the case for me. Instead of vacationing in an exotic city and popping bottles with my man or my girls, I was glued to my living room couch watching Grey's Anatomy reruns.

"Come on bitch, what we doing? I will not let you sit in here and be sad on your birthday," Tyra argued as she stood in front of the large flat screen that was mounted on the wall, intentionally blocking it.

Her words vibrated in my ears. They were triggering. My brows dipped and my solemn expression hardened. I was supposed to be sad. Being anything else didn't feel right. It pissed me off when motherfuckers downplayed the grief process and how long it should last. *"Death is a part of life." "You can't stay sad forever."* I'd heard all that bullshit, and it always angered me. In my opinion, grief was forever. You never got over losing people. You just learned to adjust. Learned to be less sad.

I hadn't long hit the year anniversary of my son's death, so I had every right to be depressed. I never asked for pity and I damn sure never asked anyone to try and cheer me up. I just wanted to hurt in peace. Wasn't I entitled to that? Unfortunately, sulking in peace would never happen with Tyra as my best friend. All the thoughts swirling in my mind didn't apply to her. She was a true friend for real. Actually, more like my sister. She'd never left my side through the darkest of times and she refused to leave my side today. Just five minutes ago, she showed up at my door with a cake, balloons, ice cream and a gift. A black face Movado watch that I'd been saying I wanted. I loved it and had expressed my gratitude and appreciation; however, I now felt a twinge of irritation for her. Although she was a good friend, her words were still triggering.

Feeling the intensity of my glare, Tyra plopped down on the couch beside me and threw her arm around my torso and squeezed me tight.

"I'm sorry best. I didn't mean it like that."

She kissed the side of my face.

"I know you're still hurting. I just want you to try to at least enjoy your birthday."

She paused while I continued to sit silently.

"Just step outside of your pain for a minute and try to have a good day. I know they are far and few between, but it's your birthday. Ya boy was all about a good time. He would want to see his mama have fun."

I continued to sit quietly but a faint smile did manage to tug at the corners of my mouth. Losing a child changed you. It changed your mood, your purpose, your will to live. You could have five children but losing one made you feel dead inside, even though you still had the four others. My babygirl was suffering. She wasn't being abused and she still had everything she needed but I knew I hadn't been giving her the time and love she needed. The affection she craved.

I felt guilty. Seeing her play alone. Watch tv alone. Even eat alone. It was like she'd lost her mom and now just had an emotionless caretaker. I'd been doing better with her and trying to get back to being the nurturing mother she deserved but I had a long way to go.

I'd seen a therapist, but that shit didn't help so I stopped going. The only thing that kept me from opening up my wrist with a razor blade was the fact that I still had that little girl to look out for. She deserved a mother.

I knew Tyra always had my best interest. It wasn't about partying or going out and shaking ass. She really wanted me to try to live and function better. I worked, but other than that, I stayed in the house. I had a man but was close as fuck to losing him. Since our argument last week, I'd barely seen much of him.

Confronting him that night didn't seem to do shit but push him further away. He hadn't even attempted to celebrate my birthday. Hadn't even mentioned it. To be honest, he'd probably forgotten it.

"Do you remember that time you threw Wave's 21st birthday party here?" Tyra asked, pulling me out of my thoughts and breaking the silence in the room.

I smiled. How could I ever forget it? My thoughts drifted back to that day.

"Quan couldn't have been no more than thirteen," she said.

"And he begged to help out with the party because he knew that we were gonna be acting like plum dumb fools," I finished, reminiscing about the day.

"This was back when he swore that he was a content creator and was doing his 'day in the life' videos. He would videotape any and everybody he could. That one was 'celebrate my aunties 21st birthday with me'. He knew he was going to get views because we all act crazy when we get to drinking. And to make sure of that shit, Quan double-spiked the punch with Zalo's Tequila."

My head rolled back as I laughed at some of the shit my son used to do for content.

"And sat them laced-ass brownies out for everyone to eat. Snuck his friends Mikey and Rashad in the house and then proceeded to record that shit and post it all over Snap."

"Girl! A time was had!" Tyra laughed. "Cross faded like a motherfucker! Them brownies with that

Tequila on top of that Vodka had us fuckeddddddd up!"

"And shitty!" I added, remembering how one of the girls that attended had shit on herself while drunk.

"Those three little fuckers laughed so hard at us that they were in here rolling around on the floor crying." Tyra continued.

Although that was a good memory, tears formed in my eyes. I missed my son so badly. Longed for him. Tears slipped down my face but that didn't stop Tyra from continuing. She too had become emotional. Her voice cracked as she spoke.

"The point I'm trying to make E, is go out for your birthday and have fun. Laugh and cut up for your boy. Let him see you have a good time, just like he would want you to."

I let out a low emotional sigh. Wiping away the tears from my eyes, I smiled and looked over at her. She always came through.

"I'll do it for Quan," I said softly.

"Yes!" Tyra shrieked, jumping from the chair and grabbing my arm.

"Let's go bitch. I already got in touch with Wave and Miracle, so they're meeting us out."

"Let's go fuck it up for Quan!"

I smiled and stood to my feet. I had no idea how the night was going to go, but I vowed to go out and make the most of it.

~

*T*he Blu Bar was one of the hottest spots in Baltimore city. It was a restaurant/hookah bar/lounge/sports bar. It wasn't like all the other bar clubs that just had some strobe lights and loud music. This place was a club with ADHD. The owner of the spot had a lot of ideas of what he or she wanted it to be when figuring out a concept. It served so many purposes and catered to several different vibes. Whether you desired a low-key vibe or a more turned up night, you could find it there.

The huge space was broken down into sections. On one side of the The Blu Bar, there were several pool tables and half a dozen televisions for sports enthusiasts. In the back of the bar there was music playing and a dance floor for those that wanted the true party experience. There was a deck outside for hookah and smoking for those that wanted to chill and vibe. And there was seating all throughout for those that got hungry or simply wanted to stop in and have a bite to eat.

The place was upscale, and even though they played R&B and Hiphop, still catered to an elite crowd. Ballers, dealers, social media influencers, and regular folk with good paying jobs frequented the establishment. The menu price kept the broker's out, which in my opinion was why the place seemed to be sticking around for a while.

What made The Blu Bar unique was when you walked in, the place was illuminated in a deep hue of blue. The staff wore blue button ups, and they even had a special drink called the Blu Devil.

"This shit packed," I said, after showing ID and walking through the door.

That was another thing. You had to be twenty-one to enter and they didn't play about that. Security was tight and if that ID wasn't right, they weren't letting you in.

"Hell yeah, it's packed," Tyra agreed. "It's Saturday, so I expected it to be.

After being scanned with a metal detector and having our bags checked, Tyra and I proceeded into the club. While she peered around and led the way, I followed closely behind. From the outside, the place was huge, but from the inside, it was gigantic. Before it became The Blu Bar, it used to be an old warehouse. Once an eyesore, the space was now vibrant and beautiful.

"Miracle and Wave already here. They got a booth in the back," Tyra said, turning over her shoulder to talk to me briefly.

I nodded even though she had already turned back around and couldn't see my response. As I walked, I couldn't help but take in the club's design. It was nice before, but it was even better now. It appeared to have been renovated. Chic and posh is how I would describe it. Upon walking in, there were black booths that ran along both sides of the wall, tables in the middle and multiple bars. Blue walls. Shiny black floors.

After walking a little further, I spotted my cousin,

Miracle waving to get our attention. She was seated near the back, close to the dance floor. Music blared through the speakers and got louder the closer we got. I spotted Wave but because she was too busy with her head buried in her phone, she didn't even notice us approaching.

"Hey cuzzo!" Miracle said jumping up out of the booth and embracing me.

I hugged her tall frame tightly, inhaling her citrusy scent.

Wave looked up and became all teeth.

"Hey!" I spoke.

"Happy birthday love!" Wave crooned as soon as Miracle released me.

"Thank you," I replied happily, before leaning into her outstretched arms for a hug.

I still didn't feel up to being out, but I was going to put on a smile and try to have a good time. I was still genuinely happy to see them.

"You look good!" she said after we broke our embrace.

Wave and Miracle gave me an approving once over while I stood there and grinned. I'd kept it simple in a black, long sleeved bodycon dress that squeezed my hips. I threw on a pair of white gold diamond hoops to complete the look. I didn't do too much because I didn't want to stand out. Something I already struggled with.

"I see you get ya style from ya baby sis," Wave joked.

"You were hiding in my closet when I got dressed?" she

asked, sliding out of the booth to show me that we were dressed nearly identical.

I smiled and gave a 'get the fuck outta here look'. She too wore a black bodycon dress. While mine stopped at the knee, hers appeared to stop at the bottom of her ass cheeks.

"Girl, you've copied my style yo' whole life," I joked back.

Wave ushered me into the booth beside her, while Tyra sat on the outside of the booth next to Miracle. I was cool with the seating. Tyra and I worked together, and Wave called me every damn day. I was low-key excited to sit across from my favorite cousin and chop it up.

"We ordered appetizers, and I got us a round of Blu Devils," Wave said.

I didn't protest. I simply went with the flow. While half of Wave's attention went to her phone, Miracle, Tyra and I began to talk about hair, the shop, and neighborhood gossip. We'd all grown up in the same area and attended the same school, so we knew all the same people.

Service was slow. It took us nearly fifteen minutes to get our drinks and another twenty-five to get four appetizers. Our waitress had an attitude and when she finally did get our appetizers to us, they weren't even hot like we expected them to be.

"This shit isn't even fucking hot," Miracle complained as soon as we all began digging into the food.

She sampled the dip while pushing one of the baskets of wings from in front of her and closer towards me.

"Girl. Please just eat the shit and don't give these people no problems," Tyra said, not wanting to hear Miracle's mouth.

Everyone knew how Miracle could get. Tyra had always been the practical, levelheaded one, while me, Wave, and Miracle were all feisty by nature. The two of them more so.

Although we were all from the same neighborhood, Miracle and Tyra's sole connection was me. They were cool but neither were each other's cup of tea. Miracle was loud, ghetto and quick-tempered while Tyra was the opposite. She had her loud moments, but she was toned down compared to everyone else. I wasn't loud but I would pop my shit whenever I felt like it.

"Girl please."

Miracle dismissed Tyra's request as quickly as it left her lips.

"I'm not paying for this cold bullshit. Wings hard as bricks and dip old and cold like my dead granny. Excuse me! Waitress!" she called out, waving her hands in the air to get her attention.

Wave laughed while Tyra turned her head in embarrassment.

"Yes? Is everything okay?" our waitress asked, returning to the table from the closest bar area.

She was a pretty, black girl. Young. Maybe in her

mid-twenties. She looked like she could've been a college student.

"No. Everything is not okay. Our food is cold, and we waited damn near a half hour to get it."

"I'm sorry, I can get everything made fresh for you," she said.

She was doing her best to be pleasant, but her brows had unconsciously dipped while her forehead crinkled. She was irritated.

"Was it not fresh when you brought it out?" Wave chimed, giving her a confused look.

I sighed internally. The two of them together were about to make a small situation, a big one.

"I'm confused what we waited thirty minutes for. Did you just snatch some old shit off the counter or something?" Miracle continued to question.

"Ma'am, I understand you're frustrated but why would I do that? The kitchen is backed up and we're short staffed. I grabbed it as soon as I saw it."

"Girl go get the manager," Miracle said smacking the tabletop of the booth. "Because your attitude is bad, and I don't got time. I'm hungry and I been done reached over and folded yo' little ass up."

The waitress mumbled something under her breath but quickly walked off. She didn't even bother to pick up the trays of appetizers we'd picked over.

I gave Miracle a 'cut it the fuck out' look.

"Stop it," I told her.

"Fuck that E. This shit ain't cheap."

She waved her hand over the table pointing at the food. Although she was rude as hell, she was right.

Our drinks were $15 a piece while the wings were $22 a basket and the dip was $18 a basket. The food was good, but it was definitely overpriced. To be delivered cold, was ridiculous.

After waiting for another ten minutes, a man that walked with the sway and swagger of a boss walked up. He had to be the manager. He had his head turned to the side as he gently barked out orders to a few staff members. When he turned his head to our table and my eyes landed on his face, all I could think was *'my have the tables turned'.* The world seemed to get smaller and smaller by the day as I stared into the man's familiar face. I was about to give his mean ass a taste of his own medicine.

"How you ladies doing this evening. I'm the owner. What's going on?"

"Kyson?" Tyra asked, remembering the handsome, but evil man that gave us a hard time in the shop the week before.

He smiled and that's when I noticed something was off. This was the same man though. I was certain.

I think.

"Actually, I'm Kobra. Kyson is my brother. He's the other owner."

"Y'all twins or something?" Tyra asked.

He flashed another handsome smile.

"We are."

"Well damn," I mumbled.

I was shocked in several ways. It wasn't often you saw identical twins in Baltimore and it damn sure wasn't often that two black brothers owned the hottest club in the city.

"We the same height but his hairs a little longer, he's got a slight gap in his teeth, and a scar on his face."

I was actually surprised at how friendly Kobra was. He was the absolute opposite of his brother. Their energies were also different. While Kobra was sexy, Kyson was dangerously sexy. He had a darkness about him that was slightly magnetic. Unfortunately, his attitude distracted you from that magnetism. Kobra gave hood nigga energy, but Kyson gave off boss. His vibe screamed that he wasn't to be fucked with.

"Kyson's actually here." He looked over his shoulder as if he was somewhere back there. "Would y'all rather speak with him?" he asked.

"Hell no," I said quickly, nearly spitting out my Blu Devil.

I didn't have time to deal with Kyson's foolishness. Besides, if he was anything here like he was in the shop, he wasn't going to do shit but make our experience worse.

Kobra chuckled at my response.

"My brother isn't too bad. Probably caught him on a bad day."

I didn't give a fuck about none of that and the hard eye roll I gave made that clear.

"Your waitress said you complained about your food being cold."

"It *was* cold," Miracle stated bluntly.

"I apologize for that. I know it's no excuse, but we are short staffed. My brother and I don't usually work the floor but hiding in the office or at home doesn't seem fair when our staff is overwhelmed. I'm gonna comp your appetizers and drinks for the inconvenience, and I'll get you some hot food redelivered."

"That would be beautiful," Wave said, finally speaking. "Especially because it's my sister's here birthday."

She pointed at me while she smiled. I, in turn, flushed red from embarrassment. I nudged her knee with mine.

"Really?" he asked.

"Yep," Tyra co-signed while Miracle nodded.

"Well then, happy birthday. It's an honor that you chose to spend it here. We'll definitely take care of you. I'm gonna send you over something special," he assured.

"Mmmmm hhhmmm. And don't forget about us," Miracle said, eyeing Kobra lustfully.

Kobra chuckled and flashed that signature smile.

"Your drinks and food will be out shortly."

Kobra walked off and the girls squealed.

"Damn he fine!" Miracle exclaimed, licking her lips and cocking her head to the side to look at me. "Did you see him?"

"Yes." I grinned. "I saw him."

"And you say he got a twin?" Miracle asked.

"Yeah, but girl that nigga is rude as hell. You don't want him," I assured her.

Kyson was nice to look at but I highly doubted that he would be good for anything else other than that.

"Shit if I don't," Miracle replied while she rocked her hips from side to side like she was ready to drop down and get her eagle on right at the table.

Both Wave and Tyra laughed at Miracle's antics while we swallowed down our drinks. I could tell Miracle was on one. Her and my sister had ridden together and according to a whisper from Wave, she was lit when she stopped by her apartment to pick her up.

Another ten minutes or so passed when brand new appetizers arrived from a new waitress. As she placed the dishes on the table, I could see light steam coming from the tops. She sat everything down, told us to 'enjoy' before scurrying off.

"Okayyyyy," Tyra sang. "I see Kobra got us right."

"He sure did," Wave cosigned, grabbing a nacho and digging into one of the spinach dips.

I smiled in satisfaction and went to do the same, but we now had a fresh round of drinks approaching. A huge grin stretched across Tyra's face as she stole peeks in my direction.

Him. He was a sight to behold earlier that day and boy was he a sight now. Even sexier than before. I could attest to the fact that he cleaned up nice. He too wore a blue button up to match the aesthetic. Only the top two buttons had been left undone. His caramel chest peeking out. Same braids neatly braided against his head. Handsome face, brooding eyes, and that dark, dangerously masculine energy. He would've been perfect if he kept quiet and never opened his mouth.

"Round of Blu Devil's on the house," he said, before unloading the drinks onto the table in front of us.

His energy was nothing like it was days prior. This seemed to be a different man. He sat an extra glass next to my complimentary drink. A much smaller one.

"Double shot of Tequila for the birthday girl."

He smiled and winked at me causing my coochie to jump a little.

"Thank you," I said, smiling coyly.

"How's the food this time ladies?" he asked, making eye contact with each girl one by one.

He turned his head slightly and it was then that I saw the scar on his cheek that his brother spoke of. I'd overlooked it before, no longer interested in his appearance after he started talking shit. He was a lot more pleasant this time though and I now found him intriguing.

"You Kyson?" Miracle asked, while everyone else was murmuring 'good' in response to his question.

"I am." He turned his head to Tyra and then looked at me. "I think we got off on a bad start a few days ago. My brother pointed you out and I wanted to come over and speak to the both of you on a more positive note."

Tyra smiled, while I rolled my eyes once more. If that was his version of an apology, it was weak as fuck.

"It's all good," Tyra replied.

"You and your brother fine as fuck," Miracle said randomly with zero shame.

I almost spit my drink out. They were, but Miracle's brashness always surprised me. I should've gotten used to it by now. It did however, cut some of the tension hovering over the table.

"Thank you," Kyson chuckled. "Likewise."

He looked around the table and then his eyes landed on me and stayed there.

"Especially you. Easton right."

I smirked but lowered my gaze away from his. I hesitated to speak. That Blu Devil had kicked in and I was liable to say some shit. Kyson was so damn fine, and I had to keep reminding myself that I was a married woman, *and* he had been a rude, piece of shit the week before.

"Thank you," I choked out.

"You're welcome. I'll send out another round. I want the birthday beauty to have a good time. Your money's no-good tonight. My way of apologizing and helping you celebrate."

"You don't have —"

"Thank you!" Wave said loudly, cutting me off.

She nudged me with her elbow while Kyson stood there gazing at me like I was a mystery he was trying to figure out.

"I insist, and you ladies are welcome. Be sure to have a good night," he said, before turning around and walking off.

Everyone waited quietly until he got far enough away so as not to overhear us.

"Bitch! Are you crazy?" Miracle laughed. "Don't you

ever try and turn down no free shit. It's clear as day that nigga want you. Or think you fly. Either way, take advantage of that shit."

"Girl that nigga guilty for acting like an ass the other day. Plus, bitch I ain't no freeloader," I quipped.

"Call it what you want. It's your birthday. That's what you supposed to do!"

"Ya heard!" Wave cosigned, reaching across the table to hi-five Miracle.

~

We were on our fourth round of drinks when I realized that those Blu Devils were no joke. I'd been laughing hysterically, eating good and had even got up a few times to shake my ass. I had to admit that I was enjoying myself, and while it was no exotic island, I was satisfied with the way my transition into year thirty was turning out.

I'd never been a big drinker but tonight I welcomed it. Alcohol took my mind off my troubles and allowed me to just be. It helped me escape the pain of having problems that even a big ass bank account couldn't fix. Knowing that I would never be able to talk, laugh or see my son again was the hardest pill I ever had to swallow. The alcohol didn't make me forget the fact; it just helped me numb it. Helped distract me from the pain I felt. It was the reason I had stopped drinking completely after my son's death. I wanted to feel everything.

I found solace in the fact that Quan would have wanted to see me having fun, so I didn't regret doing so. Usually, I avoided things that give me an inkling of joy. I didn't feel like I deserved it. Tonight, was different. Tyra's pep talk had really clung to me.

She'd also given me a speech earlier that week on stressing about Zalo and she was right. I didn't deserve how he'd been acting, even though I'd almost convinced myself that I did. He'd come back home since our fight, but I'd been seeing less and less of him. He assured me that we would go back to how we were as soon as I was ready. However, me not having sex with him shouldn't have stopped him from calling or celebrating my thirtieth birthday with me. It left a bad taste in my mouth and a bad impression on those that loved me. Thankfully, none of them argued about his behavior; they instead focused on making sure that I enjoyed myself.

"So, we ride out for the day. DC. You know … a little day trip and shit. We go to Mastro's, and this nigga insists on going in a fucking Under Armour outfit and some black Air Force ones."

The fact that we were all drunk made Wave's story about her latest dating disaster, even funnier. She was naturally funny and always had some crazy ass story to tell.

"Un uhh girl." Miracle shook her head and frowned. "Under Armour? At Mastro's."

"Yeah girl. They wear that shit around here like it's fucking designer," she continued in disgust. "We'd already made reservations, and he knew it was going to be fine dining so why the fuck he didn't have shit else with him but Under Armour?"

We all laughed while she continued theatrically.

"You know they didn't let us in with that shit. I was so embarrassed. Then we get back to the hotel and he thought he was gonna get some. Girl, that nigga went and took a shower, I took a few hundred out his wallet and called a fuckin' Uber back to Baltimore."

"What I tell you about doing shit like that?" I turned and stared her down.

Even though I was drunk, I couldn't help but be in big-sister, protector mode.

"Girl that nigga a lame that work a corporate job downtown. He ain't gon' do shit," she laughed.

That revelation brought a sense of peace to me. Wave was young and dumb, but she wasn't green. She knew not to steal from a hood nigga. Where we were from, a few hundred dollars could cost your life.

"Still. Stop doing that."

Wave dismissed me jokingly with her hand. She always teased that I was like a nagging mother.

"I'm gonna go smoke a cigarette outside on the patio. Y'all coming?" Miracle asked, already digging in her purse for the nasty cancer-causing stick.

"No. I'll wait 'til y'all get back," Tyra said frowning slightly.

Miracle noticed the look on Tyra's face and returned it with an eye roll. She always expressed that she felt like Tyra thought she was better than them.

"I wasn't really asking you," she said to Tyra. "I know Wave will come with me."

She was right. Wave was already climbing out the booth and I was right behind her. The liquor had my head in a drunken spin, and I needed to move around.

"I'm gonna run to the bathroom and then meet y'all outside," I told Miracle and Wave. "I need some fresh air."

EGYPT TESTAYE

*B*enny had been blowing my phone up for the past twenty-four hours like he'd lost his damn mind. Just as I anticipated, he missed my imaginary birthday, which ultimately gave me the reason I needed to send his ass packing. He'd been ignoring me the entire day, despite me blowing his phone up. Had my birthday been real, he would have hit me a few days later talking about how he had been tied up. I didn't even let it drag out that long. The text had been simple.

Really Benny. On my birthday. I can't do this shit any more.

I expected him to take it bad, but not this bad. Benny had called my phone over fifty times, texted me a dozen, and had even left me several voicemails. That didn't include the voice messages he'd sent and the calls from the blocked and unknown numbers. He'd started off apologetic; he eventually went to begging, and now he was on the angry stage.

I didn't give a fuck about none of that. I was going to change my number and my routine, so I didn't have to see Benny's big, fat-ass face another day in my life. He wasn't the first nigga I'd skated on. I had a big, boss nigga out in Detroit that I'd left high and dry and a scamming ass nigga in Atlanta that I'd rolled on. If I could leave them, he was no exception. That's what I did. Made niggas fall in love, got what I wanted from them and kept it moving. There was always a bigger fish to catch, and I was the fisherman. My goal was to land one of those ball players, but that shit didn't work out.

Instagram had led me to Baltimore. I'd seen a few bitches that I followed that were living large by fucking with a few niggas from a gang called BMM. The Baltimore Money Mob. Those hoes were mediocre in my eyes, so I wasted no time, catching a flight and heading out to Maryland to shine amongst a bunch of chicks that didn't hold a torch to me. Benny was my first catch and he'd been a good one, except for the fact that he was married and wanted a bitch to play house. I wasn't for none of that, so it was time to abort the mission.

Benny had several reasons to be mad at me, but he'd settled on being mad at the fact that I was out on a date with another man. I swiped money from his wallet while he showered and had called him every fat name under the sun, yet he hadn't mentioned any of that. He instead, chose to show his big, black, country ass because he couldn't stand the thought of me being on a date, skinning and grinning with another nigga. What were the odds of me picking the same spot that Benny was at? I definitely hadn't done it on purpose.

"Fuck is you doing?" Benny asked, while I sat in the booth across from my petrified looking date.

"What does it look like?" I asked, trying to play it cool. His size was naturally intimidating; however, were in a highly public place so I knew he wasn't about to do shit.

His eyes glistened into mine. I could tell that he was hurt but I didn't care. I just wanted him to get the fuck out of my face and leave me alone.

"Babe get up and let me talk to you for a minute," Benny said, ignoring the blatant disregard for his feelings or pride.

"I'm not your babe, and there's nothing to talk about. Where's your wife? Isn't it y'all anniversary?" I asked, rolling my eyes.

I was dead wrong, but I had to keep this shit about him. I had to continue making him believe that he was the reason that I was out living my best life.

"You couldn't be with me on my birthday weekend, so I got someone else to be with me."

I swallowed the lump that had grown in my throat. Benny was huge. Well over six foot. Well, over three hundred pounds. His lip was now trembling in anger and his chest had begun to rise and fall. His presence was threatening, and I would be a liar to say I wasn't intimidated. I was actually getting kind of scared.

"Egypt." Benny paused and glared at me. "I'm not going to ask you again. Get up and come talk to me."

I took a deep breath and looked at my date, Rodney. He was a simp that I had met about a month ago. He was my in-between until I found a new nigga.

"I'm sorry. Like I was saying. What are you getting?"

I looked down at my menu while Rodney continued to sit silently.

"Egypt get the fuck up," Benny said again, as I suspected he would.

"You still standing here?" I asked him, looking up from my menu.

"You think I'm fuckin' play with you!" Benny roared, taking me aback.

He grabbed me by the arm and then yanked me out the booth so forcefully, he nearly dislocated my shit. Instead of holding onto me, he hurled me to the floor. I landed on my backside and fell a few feet away.

"Are you crazy?" I screamed in embarrassment.

I groaned from the pain but quickly shook it off. Scrambling to my feet, I went to swing but went hurling backward when Benny backhanded me back down to the floor. My lip tore and I felt the blood begin to run.

"No bitch! You're the crazy one. You obviously don't know who the fuck I am! Who the fuck you think you talking to like that?" he growled, approaching me like a raging bear.

Fury flickered in his eyes while fear flashed in mine. I looked towards the booth at Rodney, but he was sliding out of the seat and running full speed toward the door. I was about to talk some more shit but the blood running from my lips reminded me that probably wasn't a good idea. That was confirmed when Benny leaned down and grabbed a fistful of my hair.

"Benny please," I begged, now up off the floor because he had used my hair to lift me.

"Shut the fuck up. You bring yo' ass in a well-known spot. A place you know I be at. And disrespect me. I should take you out back and kill yo' mafuckin ass."

My head was cocked to the side as Benny maintained his grip, shaking me every few seconds for good measure. I looked into his face and a wave of terror washed over me. The same eyes that usually held warmth for me, were now dark and cold.

"Benny please let me go," I sobbed.

My eyes darted around the establishment as people stared at us. The place was packed but nobody said a word. I was mortified.

"Shut the fuck up," he said, before striking me in the face again with his open hand.

My ears rang from the impact. His hands were so large, the slap felt like a punch.

"Hey bud! Chill!" some random white man said, coming to my aid.

He too was a big guy, although a little smaller than Benny.

"Let her go. She's a woman and you're a —"

Before the man could finish his sentence, Benny had dropped me to the ground, pulled out his gun and cracked the man over the head with it.

"Where the hell are my keys, Lola?" I barked, my eyes narrowing as she lay across the bed like she didn't have a care in the world.

Naked and smug, she twirled a piece of her hair between her fingers, her expression blank, but I knew better. Lola wasn't innocent. She wasn't even good at pretending to be. The smirk tugging at the corner of her lips told me everything I needed to know. She'd hidden them again. That was the stupid shit she did. She thought her little antics were cute, but it was starting to piss me off.

I rubbed my temples, my patience wearing thin. "I know you hid them. Go get my shit. I gotta go."

She yawned, her mouth wide as if she could care less about anything I'd said.

"Why you always blaming me? Maybe you lost them. You ever think of that?" she said in her high-pitched voice.

"I ain't lose shit."

She did this every time I tried to leave. The bitch was like quicksand—always pulling me in, no matter how much I fought. And the crazy part? I let her. Every. Single. Time.

Lola wasn't shit. She knew it. I knew it. Hell, she knew that I knew it. But she also knew I wasn't going anywhere. Why? Her sex ... fire. Our chemistry ... unmatched. She could cook, clean, and blow a nigga's brain's out from the grip of her lips. She had a nigga open. So open that I cut off all my other jump off's and made her my primary side bitch. Clearly, I had fucked up.

Lola had the good qualities that I mentioned. But her bad ones, I was slowly beginning to see, outweighed the good ones. She was sneaky, petty, and lived for social media drama. She loved posting subliminals that made people question what I had going on. And even though I couldn't prove it, I was sure she was fucking other niggas.

She didn't work but somehow stayed dripping in luxury—designer bags, red-bottom heels, the works. She drove a G-Wagon and lived in an apartment almost as big as the one I shared with Easton. She partied every weekend like it was her birthday, yet she had the nerve to press me about leaving Easton for her. I couldn't be with a bitch that was for the streets. That wasn't happening, and she knew it.

"I'm not playing with you. Get your ass up and find my keys before I—"

"Before you what?" She cocked her head to the side, daring me to finish the sentence.

I sighed and pinched the bridge of my nose, trying to keep my temper in check. I didn't have time for this. Easton's birthday was today, and I'd completely forgotten about it. I'd been reminded when I scrolled through social media and saw Wave's Instagram post from a couple of hours ago. There Easton was, out at The Blu Bar, looking good in a black dress that hugged her curves. She was smiling, but I knew her well enough to see the pain behind that smile.

I felt guilty as fuck. I loved her—God, I loved her—but lately, we'd been on opposite sides of a war we didn't even know how to fight. She'd pulled away from me, drowning in her grief, and I didn't know how to reach her anymore. I'd let my frustration drive me straight into Lola's bed. It was supposed to be a quick, temporary fix. But somehow, I'd gotten caught up with the bitch and she was making a mess out of my life.

"Yo, I'm not gon' ask you again," I told her.

She rolled onto her back, stretching like a cat before propping herself up on her elbows.

"I didn't touch your keys," she said, her tone as nonchalant as ever. Then she spread her legs, her freshly waxed skin glistening in the dim bedroom light. She ran a finger over her folds, slow and deliberate, before smirking at me. "Why you in such a rush anyway? Come here. Kiss it one last time before you go."

I clenched my jaw and looked away, but it was too

88

late. My dick was already hard, betraying me the way it always did around her. She knew exactly what she was doing. Lola had me figured out, and that pissed me off almost as much as it turned me on.

"I can't," I muttered, though my voice didn't sound convincing even to my own ears. "I got shit to do."

"You always got shit to do," she said, sitting up and swinging her legs off the bed. She stood and sauntered toward me, her hips swaying with every step. "But you always end up here, Zalo. With me."

She dropped to her knees in front of me and reached for my belt. My breath hitched as her fingers quickly fumbled with the buckle.

"Stop. I gotta go."

My voice was a weak protest, but I didn't move.

"You sure you don't want to stay?" she asked, her voice dripping with sweetness as she slid my pants down. "Just a little longer?"

My boxers followed, and I groaned as the cool air and anticipation of the act hit me. She licked her lips, and my resolve crumbled. By the time her mouth wrapped around me, I was done. My head fell back, and a deep moan escaped my throat.

"Shit," I muttered, stepping back and following onto the bed while she worked her magic.

I hated myself for this. For letting her win again. But damn if I could stop her. Damn if I even wanted to. The keys could wait. Easton … could wait.

KYSON MCCARTER

$\mathcal{T}$he sound of gunshots stopped me in my tracks. "What the fuck," I mumbled as my heart began to race.

It wasn't fear that was driving the speed, it was adrenaline. I was a hood nigga so when I heard gunshots, that meant it was time to ride. Being in the restaurant forced me to rethink my next move. I was standing in the kitchen, loading a serving tray to run orders out onto the floor but immediately put it down when I heard the sounds.

"Lock in!" I yelled out to the entire kitchen staff.

We had procedures in place for shit like this. We were in Baltimore, and I forbade my staff from trying to be heroes of any sort. They'd all been instructed and trained to take cover in the event some shit popped off. This was one of those times. We didn't know the patrons that frequented The Blu Bar and weren't about to die to save them motherfuckers either.

I grabbed my gun off my hip and gripped it in my hand. My brother was on the floor. Until I could confirm his safety, I wasn't locking in. I ran towards the door before any of the staff could lock it but stopped in my tracks when I saw Kobra run inside.

"You good?" I asked, doing a brief scan of his body for any injuries.

When I realized he was, I waited for him to update me on what he'd seen. His eyes were wide, he was breathing heavy, and he was staring at me like he had something to say.

"Yeah, I'm straight," he said, still out of breath. "It's Benny dumb ass. He beat up one of his side bitch's at one of the tables and some white guy tried to break it up. They got to fighting and either the gun went off or Benny fired on him. I don't know for sure yet. Shit crazy out there."

The mention of Benny's name caused my jaws to tighten. I never cared much for the nigga. He'd done business with my father since moving to Baltimore from Florida as a teen. He was loud, country, obnoxious, and thought he knew everything. I was a little confused about how he'd gotten himself in a domestic situation. I'd actually seen him an hour earlier sitting at a table with his crew *and* his wife. Him getting out of character for a side-bitch showed how weak the nigga truly was. But for him to act out in our place of business demonstrated how stupid he was as well. The shit made my blood boil.

Since he'd became a member of BMM, he'd made

my father a lot of money. However, the more money he made, the more reckless he became. He'd been a liability and the only reason I'd spared him this long was because of our father. All that was about to change.

"Fuck," I muttered, looking at Kobra. "We gotta do damage control *and* crowd control."

Kobra nodded and then headed back out the doors onto the floor. I followed him.

"You hit the sports section," I instructed.

While he went right, I went left, heading towards the dance area and outside patio. The sound of screaming, shattering glass, and chairs and tables being knocked over rang in my ears. Kobra already knew that we needed to find Benny. The last thing we needed was him to get snatched up by the cops and they tie him to us. To the city, we were legit businessmen. To the streets, we were the head of The Baltimore Money Mob, a vicious gang of drug dealers and killers. Although he technically worked for us, Benny had a reputation that we couldn't be affiliated with publicly.

His actions would definitely have consequences. He'd knowingly brought his fat ass in our establishment and caused turmoil. When the night was over, we would probably have to worry about: paying off the bitch he beat up, the white guy he attacked, erasing video footage, lying to police, and paying lawsuits to anyone hurt while trying to flee the building.

The people running, twisting, turning, and moving to get out the way, had me feeling like I was in a war zone. I had nearly tripped over an overturned chair in the middle of the floor when a woman ran right into me. I grabbed her waist to catch her from falling.

"You okay?" I asked, pulling her back some to get a look at her once she was able to gain her balance.

I released her. It was Easton, and she was a hysterical mess. She looked like she was in the middle of a mental health crisis. Her hair was wild, her eyes were wide, and tears streaked her face.

"I can't find my girls!" she screamed frantically. "I gotta make sure they're okay! I gotta find my girls! Help me please!" she cried, her arms angled and hands up as if pleading with me.

She held her phone tightly in her hand while she cried.

"Hey— Hey —Hey— Listen," I shushed her. "Slow down okay. Calm down for just a second."

My words seemed inappropriate, especially with all the turmoil erupting around us. I held her by her shoulders while she inhaled and exhaled deep breaths.

"I'll help you find them, but for now, I need you to calm down so I can get you somewhere safe," I told her.

The gunshots had stopped but the stampede of people running around frantically was just as if not more dangerous. I stared into Easton's eyes as she continued to try and calm herself. Something about seeing her frantic and scared made me reprioritize. She was now my main concern and finding Benny had been pushed to the backburner. Kobra would handle it.

"Let's go," I said firmly.

I was going to take her to my office on the other

side of the building. We just had to get through a sea of people to get there. I grabbed her hand and began steering her through the commotion. Easton's hand gripped mine like her life depended on it. Her body trembling as we dodged broken glass, overturned tables, and running, screaming patrons.

After a bunch of pushing and shoving we made it to the rear of the building. I pushed open the door to my office and ushered her inside. The room was sleek, decked out in rich shades of blue and black. Black leather chairs sat in front of a polished ebony desk, while a plush navy rug covered the floor. The walls were adorned with abstract art that matched the club's high-end, moody vibe.

"Sit down," I ordered, locking the door behind us.

Easton looked around quickly and sank onto a nearby couch, her hands shaking as she tried to steady her breathing. Her eyes darted around the room like she couldn't believe everything was happening.

"Hey. You're good now," I said, crouching in front of her. "Nobody's getting in here."

I wasn't sure if the commotion had her riled up or the thought of being shot. Either way, the ordeal had her shook. Easton nodded, but tears brimmed in her eyes. She was back on her phone, pushing buttons and trying to call out.

"Shit," she mumbled, rubbing her temples. "I can't— I can't reach them. I don't know if they're okay! I tried to call each of them, but no one is answering."

She brought her phone back up to her face and was

about to begin dialing again. That's when her screen went black.

"Fuck!" she yelled. "It's dead."

She began to look around frantically and I could tell that she was about to really lose her shit.

"Hey," I said, my tone sharp enough to get her attention. "Try to relax. I gotchu," I reassured her.

I pulled my phone out of my pocket, put the password in and handed it to her. "Call whoever you need to."

She hesitated for a moment, her fingers trembling as she took the phone. She dialed quickly, putting it to her ear.

"Wave?" she cried as soon as the line connected. "Oh my God, where are y'all? I came from the bathroom, heard gunshots, tried to find y'all and couldn't."

I stood and turned away, giving her a little space while she talked. Her voice was frantic at first, but it softened as her sister spoke on the other end.

"I'm still at the club. I'm with Kyson. The owner."

Her sister spoke on the other end some more.

"No, I'm okay. Better now that I know y'all are okay. I'm gonna stay with him until it's safe to leave. No. No. I'll call Zalo and get him to pick me up. Yeah, I'm sure."

After talking to her sister for a little longer, Easton hung up the phone and blew a huge sigh of relief.

"They're safe," she finally said, her voice cracking with relief. "Wave, Miracle and Tyra—they made it out without getting hurt."

Her shoulders sagged, and she let out a shaky laugh, the kind that happens when you're so relieved you don't know what else to do.

"They looked for me, but…" Her voice trailed off as her eyes darted to me. "They couldn't find me, so they got out of the building."

"They had to make a choice," I said, my tone low. "They made the right one. Don't hold it against 'em."

"I don't," she whispered, wiping her face. "I'm just glad they're okay."

I nodded, watching as she made sure the call was ended and handed the phone back to me.

"Thank you," she said softly, her voice steady for the first time. She stood to her feet.

"You ain't gotta thank me."

But before I could step back, she walked toward me quickly and wrapped her arms around me, holding on tight. I froze for a second, caught off guard, but then I returned the embrace. Her warmth seeped into me, and for a moment, the chaos outside didn't exist.

Easton released me and took a step back when she felt my dick press against her. She lowered her gaze, slightly embarrassed. Her vulnerability made her even more attractive. It was hard to believe that she was the same broad that I damn near cursed out the other day. I felt bad about the shit after leaving her shop that day. I'd had a bad day and I took it out on her and her friend. Seeing her tonight, gave the opportunity to clear my conscience. It also gave me the opportunity to truly recognize the beauty she possessed. Her hair had been messy the day I'd met her. She was barefaced but still pretty. Tonight, she was dolled up with her hair down and she was sexy as fuck. While she stood in front of me awkwardly, my eyes drank all of her in.

"I'm sorry. For uh ... invading your space like that."

"You are good. Trust me, I don't mind," I said, staring into her chocolate eyes. She looked away.

"Um, can I use your phone to call my husband. So, I can get home."

"I'll make sure you get home," I told her.

"I don't think that's a good idea," she said.

"Don't matter. I'll take you home," I said with finality.

Easton nodded, her lips parting like she wanted to say something, but she stayed silent.

I wasn't about to let that nigga swoop in and end the day when I was the one that had saved it. Besides, I was low-key feeling his bitch and the less he was around, the better.

"Let's go," I said, unlocking the door. "Stay close to me."

$\sim$

The soft hum of the engine was the only sound between us as I drove Easton home. She was still quiet, staring out the window with a distant look in her eyes. Streetlights cast fleeting shadows across her face, illustrating the streaks of dried tears on her cheeks.

"You good?" I asked, breaking the silence.

I was a street dude, but it was something about her that softened a nigga up. I waited for a response while watching as her curls whipped against her cheek with every small movement she made.

She nodded, but it wasn't convincing. "Yeah, I'm good," she replied softly.

I glanced at her briefly, then back at the road. "You don't look it."

"I'll be fine," she said, her tone clipped like she was trying to convince herself.

I let it go for a moment, letting the silence settle again before speaking. "So… your girls said tonight was your birthday?"

She nodded, still looking out the window.

"Why you spend it with them and not your man?" I asked, keeping my tone casual but watching her closely out of the corner of my eye.

I really had more questions, but she was letting her guard down with me and I didn't want to fuck it up.

Her posture stiffened slightly, and she let out a short laugh, but there was no humor in it. "He's actually my husband," she reminded me. "And that's a long story," she muttered.

"I got time."

She shook her head, finally turning to look at me. "I don't want to talk about it."

That answer told me more than she probably realized. A woman like her shouldn't be out with her friends on her birthday unless something at home was broken. That would actually work in my favor. Her nigga was on bullshit, and I was about to step in.

"Fair enough," I said, keeping my voice even. But in my head, I made a note of it.

The thought of her being married didn't bother me. Not like it should've. I'd seen enough to know that rings didn't mean shit these days. I didn't know the nigga, and frankly, I didn't give a fuck. What I did care about was the fact that she was sitting in my passenger seat, looking like the weight of the world was on her shoulders. I wanted to lift that weight, to get to know her, to see that smile she was hiding.

"You live far?" I asked, changing the subject.

"No," she said softly. "Just a few more blocks."

I hadn't used my GPS since I was familiar with the downtown area.

We fell back into silence, but this time it seemed a little heavier. Like she had a lot going on and I had reminded her of it when I brought up her nigga.

We sat in silence for a little while, but it wasn't long before we were pulling up on her block. After some directions from her, I arrived in front of her building. After pulling in and going through the gate, I found a spot, put my whip in park and turned to her. The building was a swanky hi-rise. Where rich mother-fuckers lived. I could tell her little nigga wasn't doing too bad for himself.

"This it?" I asked.

She nodded, her hand already on the door handle. "Thanks for getting me home."

I nodded back, but when she opened the door and stepped out, something made me call after her.

"Easton."

She paused, turning to look at me, her expression unreadable.

"Happy birthday," I said, a smirk tugging at the corner of my mouth. 'I'll see you soon," I added so she knew that this wouldn't be our last encounter if it were up to me.

For the first time that night, she smiled—a real smile that I didn't quite expect. "Thanks, Kyson," she said softly.

I watched her walk up to the double glass doors of the building, waiting until she disappeared inside before pulling off.

As I drove away, her scent lingered faintly in the car, mixing with my thoughts. She was beautiful, complicated, and clearly dealing with more than she wanted to admit.

And I wanted to know every damn thing about her.

KOBRA MCCARTER

$\mathcal{M}$y eyes traveled up and down the frame of the pretty girl sitting on the couch in the safe room. Even in her battered and disheveled state, she was still undeniably, bad as fuck.

"Can I leave now?" she asked through smeared, swollen lips.

Judging by her appearance and impatience she was tired and completely over the night.

"No," I said bluntly. "You can leave as soon as the police are done wrapping shit up."

"What the fuck," she whined. "I don't want to be here all night."

I eyed her with a look of seriousness. Like, '*bitch, be for real*'. She was fifty percent of the reason the police were all through my shit. Half the reason why my brother and I now had thousands of dollars in damage and would likely be closed for several weeks. I wasn't one to victim blame but she was the one that brought her ass in a popular, public place with another nigga, knowing that she was fucking with a hothead like Benny. Of course, he had no right to fuck her up the way he did, but from a street perspective, she was begging for that ass whipping.

"Neither do I sweetheart but you can't leave until they wrap that shit up. You wanna press charges?" I asked her.

"No," she said softly.

"You want Benny to go to jail?" I probed further.

"Yeah, but that wouldn't benefit me ... So, no."

"Well then relax. Let them people do their little investigation, and you can roll out when they're done."

I got up from my position in one of the chairs in the room and walked over to a small bar cart in the corner. I grabbed a bottle of Tequila from the top and popped it open. After pulling a glass from the second tier of the cart, I poured a double shot.

"Here. Drink that to relax."

She needed something. She'd been restless and fidgety. Tapping her foot against the floor and fiddling with her fingers. With my arm stretched, I handed the drink to Egypt. She threw it back in one big gulp. While she swallowed the liquor down, I took a seat on the couch she sat at, just a few inches away from her.

"Thanks," she said, while making a face that indicated she wasn't fond of the taste.

I watched her as she blew out a deep breath to rid herself of the bitter bite. My eyes traveled from her lips to her hair. Her weave was tangled and sticking to the sides of her face and her makeup was streaky with eyeliner smeared around her eyes. Despite those things, she was still angelic. Still very attractive.

Egypt Testaye was a name I'd heard and a face that I'd seen around. She was what one considered a socialite. An "It Girl." By hood standards anyway. The type of bitch that I'd trick a few dollars on, if that was the type of shit that I was on. I understood why Benny was drawn to her. Had made her his. She was gorgeous. Petite, with a trending body type. She wore designer. Had thousands of followers on Instagram and had all the niggas vying for her. Heavyweights like myself included. She was the type of bitch that niggas were proud to parade around on their arm.

"What were you doing fucking with a nigga like Benny anyway?" I asked, trying to make conversation.

We'd been in the safe room, which was nothing more than a third office that we used in case we had some shit to handle. This wasn't the first time an altercation had broken out and we needed to separate some people to do damage control.

"Long story. So, to keep it short — for the money." She shrugged nonchalantly.

I nodded. At least she gave it to me honest. I couldn't stand a fake good girl.

"Respect," I said.

Egypt rolled her eyes and made a scoffing noise while shuffling her body around on the couch.

"What's all that for?" I asked, in regard to the noise.

I leaned back on the couch that we shared, interested in what she had to say.

"You said respect but do you really?" she asked eying me in contempt. I could tell that she didn't like nor appreciate the feeling of judgement. "I'm a pretty girl so I'm not fucking with a nigga unless he can do something for me. It's clear as day why I would fuck with a big, fat, bitch-ass nigga like Benny," she said, as if I was the one that had beat the shit out of her. "Love may be for me one day, but right now, it isn't. It's strictly about cash."

I could tell that she had been preached to before. Had been ostracized because of her decision to be a gold digger instead of the average woman looking for love. She was talking to me like I was the one judging her. I simply sighed and shook my head.

"Whatever shorty. I was just asking. The only reason I said 'respect' was because of the fact that you kept it real. I mean, the nigga doesn't hide the fact that he's married so, clearly, I knew the answer. I was just making small talk."

Egypt didn't bother responding. She just sat on the couch; eyes glazed over, deep in thought. I didn't bother her again after that. I instead allowed her to be in silence. After some shuffling, she curled up on the couch and soon after, she fell asleep.

An hour later, I woke her up so she could leave. The police had all gone and there was no one left to question her about the events of the night. That was always the procedure whenever Kyson and I were faced with a mess. Clear the scene and get the situation under control before the cops arrived. Whether it was the streets or business, we created our own narrative and made sure the people involved stuck to it. Situations like tonight were always the hardest to control because we didn't know the people involved.

I wasn't worried about Egypt. I let her know that I would make sure that Benny left her the fuck alone. As long as he didn't bother her again and she could peacefully go back to her life of whoring, she wouldn't talk to the police. The white guy he assaulted on the other hand, was a different story. The police were able to interview him, and he'd described Benny, the people he was with, backing up his account of what occurred. I wasn't sure how shit was going to go, but Benny was definitely going to get dealt with. He was fucking up the money and we didn't play about that money.

"Hey shorty." I grabbed Egypt's shoulder and shook her gently to wake her.

"Hey shorty, wake up."

She murmured a few things sleepily and then slowly peeled her eyes open.

"What time is it?" she mumbled.

"About four in the morning."

"I can leave?" she asked, stretching her arms and back as she sat up on the couch.

She pushed her legs out and even stretched her toes that were now bare since her heels had come off somewhere in the club. When she was done stretching, she looked off into a corner of the room as if she realized something.

"What?" I asked.

"I can't go home," she said.

"Why not?"

"I'm afraid Benny may come there. I know he will."

She stopped staring into the corner and redirected her gaze to me.

"He beat my ass in a crowded club while his wife was in the building."

She was right. Benny had damn sure caused a scene and didn't care that his wife was there. Shit, he didn't even care about the dozens of witnesses. And then to pull out a gun. He was tripping, and there was no telling what he would do to her if he came to her crib and they were alone.

"Is it okay if I just stay here?" she asked.

I shook my head. Not long ago, she was dying to leave and now she wanted to stay. I guess that nap had sobered her up and she had come to her senses.

"No," I replied flatly.

A disappointed look immediately surfaced on her face.

"The building gets locked up and there's motion sensors. You'll trigger the alarms."

Her lips began to tremble, and tears welled up in her eyes. She began to cry.

"You got any money? Maybe you can check into a hotel for a few days. Until that nigga calms down."

The hotel suggestion was more for her reassurance. I was going to deal with Benny.

She shook her head. "I lost my ID and my purse during all the commotion."

That shit was probably gone, and I wasn't about to help her look for it. It was early in the morning, and I was ready to go home. I wanted to help shorty, but I wasn't about to lose even more sleep doing so. I didn't give a fuck about Benny or his bitch problems, so letting her crash with me for the night wasn't an issue. The problem was I didn't know her well enough to let her in my crib. But it was late, and I couldn't leave her just out in the streets stranded. She had no shoes, purse, or ID. All she had was the keys to her crib and a deranged ex that I knew firsthand, would kill her ass and stuff her in his trunk if he was able to get ahold of her.

Fuck it, I thought. If the bitch tried some stupid shit, I would shoot her and anybody else.

"Look, you can crash with me. My place isn't too far away. I do want to advise though, that if you think Benny is bad, you ain't seen shit. I'm helping you, so don't be on no bullshit now *or* later."

She already knew what that entailed so I didn't bother going into details.

"Of course not," she said. "And thank you."

With that said, we were off.

EASTON BLUE

"Hey," I groaned, opening the door for Wave to enter. She was standing there with a Tupperware bowl in one hand and a small Crock-Pot cradled in the other.

"You look like shit," she remarked with a smirk as she stepped past me, her eyes flicking over my disheveled appearance. "Are you feeling any better?" she asked, despite just declaring that I looked terrible.

I dragged myself to the couch and collapsed onto it, feeling like I was moving through molasses. Every inch of my body felt like it had been run over by a truck. Wave walked into the kitchen and set the crockpot onto the countertop.

"Barely. My head's a spinning, my stomach's doing back flips... and to top it off, I think I'm still drunk. Girl last night was a fuckin' mess," I groaned.

Wave nodded in agreement as she walked into the living room and joined me on the large couch. Despite the living room being massive and there being plenty of furniture to sit on, she kicked off her shoes, plopped down beside me and snuggled right against my body.

"At least you made it home safe," she said, looking on the bright side of things. "That hangover will fade."

Silence fell over the room until Wave began speaking.

"I brought you some stew."

She smiled, still leaning against me. Her head was nestled into my breast.

"I don't know if any stew will fix this. It's a little heavy and I feel like I've been run over by a truck. My stomach probably can't handle that."

The pounding in my head was a constant drumbeat, and my stomach was still doing flips from whatever the hell was in those Blu Devils. But there was something deeper, something gnawing at me. It wasn't just the alcohol—it was the memory of last night at the club. The chaos. The fear. Kyson.

"You've been through worse. This is nothing. Is Zalo here?" she asked.

"No, why?"

"Good. Because I wanna talk about *him*."

I froze.

"*Him?*"

My pulse quickened as I slowly turned my head down towards Wave, already knowing who she meant. Kyson.

Wave raised an eyebrow and waited for me to talk.

"Yes. I wanna talk about Kyson. Old boy that tried

to make sure you had a good birthday. Same sir that made sure you got home safely."

I stared at her for a long moment, the weight of her question heavy on my chest. I sighed, running my hand through my tangled hair.

"I don't know. It's... nothing, I guess. I met him nearly a week ago at the shop. His daughter had an appointment with Tyra, but she gave her to me at the last minute. He was a dick. Rude, obnoxious. But then, he was the total opposite when we saw him at The Blu Bar." I paused. "Why are you asking me about him anyway? *I am married*," I reminded her.

Wave rolled her eyes and shook her head, clearly annoyed at the mention of Zalo.

"Girl barely. When you gonna accept the fact that Zalo's on bullshit? I get you gave him a pass to do him, but that doesn't justify the way he's been treating you. Barely coming in. Not celebrating your birthday. Do you know how we blew his phone up last night when we couldn't find you? Do you think he cared? Couldn't have, because he didn't even answer, and he damn sure didn't call us back."

I didn't reply.

"All I'm saying is, you went out last night to try to smile again. Of course, it didn't go well but you still made the effort to getting back to happy. Life is short. Yeah, he had to make some adjustments because you're grieving but you're the one that's really adjusting. If that nigga isn't trying to help you be happy, then get him the fuck outta here. Husband or no husband," she said.

I exhaled quietly. I hated when Wave tried to give me advice. I also hated when her ass made sense.

"Do you like him?" Wave asked, after a moment of intense silence.

"Like who?"

"The nigga. Kyree."

"*Kyson?*" I laughed.

"You know what I meant," she grinned.

"He finer than a motherfucker," I admitted.

"You ain't never lied," she cosigned, doing a little shake like she had goosebumps.

The image of Kyson appeared in my thoughts. His slim, thick build. Those broad shoulders and those luscious lips he liked to lick every five seconds. His voice, so silky yet masculine. In my single days, I'd definitely get a taste. Hell, I wouldn't mind one even as a married woman.

Wave leaned up, looked at me and studied me carefully.

"You do like him," she giggled.

"Whatever," I replied, shoving her playfully.

"Girl you're human. And you know I'm a firm believer in doing whatever makes you happy. If a nigga ain't acting like a husband, then he ain't a husband," she said with finality.

It was as if she was wiser than her twenty-five years and for the first time, I really thought about what she was saying. Just as I went to speak, the door opened and Zalo walked in carrying a bunch of bags. As usual, he came in noisily. His icy chains banging against each other as he walked in. He was wearing a warm smile, peering at me as if he was husband of the year.

"Wassup babe. Hey Wave."

Zalo looked good in a black Balenciaga jacket with a matching skully on.

"Zalo," Wave greeted him dryly. "Glad you finally showed up. Did you see our calls and texts about the shooting at The Blue Bar last night? Our frantic texts about not being able to find Easton?"

"Huh?" he asked, pretending to be surprised.

Just like I could tell he was lying, so could Wave; however, for some reason, he thought he had us fooled.

He dug his phone out of his pocket and scrolled through it, as if checking.

"Oh shit. I'm just seeing it now. You know my mom be having bad reception."

The bad reception part was true, but he knew damn well that he wasn't at his mom's. As soon as I got in last night, I'd called her to check on Kyllie and to see if Zalo was there. She claimed he was sleep, which I knew was a whole fucking lie. Zalo was the last to bed and first one to rise. He wasn't asleep because he wasn't there.

"Yeah whatever," she said. "Thankfully, she got home safe without you."

"I got something for you," Zalo said, ignoring Wave and looking at me.

He placed the bags on the counter. The orange and

blue bag revealed that he'd purchased me some Louis Vuitton.

"You a little late, ain't chu?" Wave asked, frowning. "Her birthday was yesterday, nigga."

"Would you mind yo' lonely ass business?" he quipped.

"Boy fuck you!" Wave yelled. "You miss her 30th birthday and then come in here with some funky ass Louis Vuitton bags. You could've bought her a car or something."

"She gotta go," Zalo said angrily throwing his hands up and walking off.

Zalo never liked to argue when he was wrong, so it was typical that he'd walk off. Paired with Wave's delivery, he knew he had no wins. Zalo exited the kitchen and shot Wave a dirty look as he strolled through the living room and to the bedroom. In return she stuck her middle finger high in the air.

I exhaled wearily. Wave was always on ten, so I should've known that as soon as he came through the door she was going to be on his ass. She didn't care how much Zalo had or what he did for our family. She never spared him. She'd curse him out and then go back to her regularly scheduled program. They had that brother-sister relationship.

"Why do you always start with him?" I groaned.

"Girl fuck him. He misses your whole birthday, and he thinks he can come up in here with some bags. Fuck a bag. He needs to *drop a bag*! Not only should you be getting a birthday gift, you should be getting an 'I'm sorry' gift. You too easy on his ass. I bet that other nigga would've come better than that. Actually, he probably wouldn't have even had to because he would've been on his shit. I can spot a boss from a mile away. That nigga got 'change ya life money'."

"Shhhhh," I demanded.

Wave popped up off the couch, clearly irritated.

"I'm gone. Tell Zalo, he can kiss my ass, and you can kiss it to if you're on his side. I love you," she said.

She leaned in, gave me a hug, and kiss on the cheek before heading toward the door. As she passed the kitchen, she stopped and turned around.

"The food in the crockpot is yours. The Tupper-ware is Zalo's. The stew has tomatoes. I know he doesn't like tomatoes. Make sure you give me my shit back too," she said, before walking out the door.

I couldn't do anything but shake my head at my crazy sister. Despite being mad at Zalo, she still took the time to be thoughtful. As simple as she was, she was just one of those people you couldn't live with but couldn't live without.

KYSON MCCARTER

"*How's* the nanny interviews coming along?" I asked my aunt, while she stood in the kitchen making dinner.

"Decent. I've got about four that I've narrowed it down to. I'm bringing them back for second interviews and once I've decided, I'll get the fingerprint checks."

I nodded in approval. Aunt Kim was always on top of things. While she adored Zoe and didn't mind caring for her, she didn't like being stuck in the house. She was no traditional older woman. Aunt Kim liked being busy and liked feeling like she had a purpose. The club was her baby. She created our signature drink, as well as the menu and had put her own special touch on everything. She was usually in and out but had been home caring for Zoe when everything went down with Benny.

Zoe had been there with us since I took her from her mother. I had my own apartment in downtown

Baltimore but since I now had Zoe around the clock, I'd been staying at the big house with Aunt Kim and Kobra. He too had another crib in the city, but just like me, he stayed at Aunt Kim's house, aka, The Big House, more.

"Have you spoken to Chelsea? She's been calling me."

I was sitting at the kitchen island when she made the statement. I looked at my aunt. She was standing there barefoot in a long, black gown with a wig on her head like she was a mob wife or some shit.

"Yeah. Same shit. She's gonna call the police. Bring her daughter back. Yada yadda yadda. Same ol' shit I ain't trying to hear."

Aunt Kim nodded in agreement.

"I saw on her story that she was out of town. Miami."

I was unmoved by the revelation. The bitch claimed she wanted her daughter back so bad but was out in Miami living her best life. Every text that I'd received from her skank ass were more about her than our child. She hadn't asked if Zoe had been to school, and she never once asked to speak to her. Zoe had to ask on her own. I did give her credit for being available when she called, but other than that, the bitch wasn't truly concerned. The truth was, I could do a better job. I'd just have to switch a few things up.

I was gone most days, handling drug business, restaurant business, or laid up somewhere with the bitches I chose to fuck with. All of that shit was about to be put on hold until I got my daughter situated.

"That's not surprising. That's all that hoe cares about."

"Well, that's the hoe you chose," Aunt Kim quipped.

I chuckled.

"What do you want me to do Auntie? Shove Zoe back up her ass?" I asked sarcastically. "What's done is done. And to keep it a buck, every mafucka I run into seems to be a hoe these days."

My auntie shot me a 'get smacked' look.

"Every motherfucker ain't no hoe these days," she said mimicking my dialogue. "You just keep chasing the same type of women. I done told you and Kobra. You need to get it together. Settle down."

I exhaled and threw up my hands in defeat. My aunt wanted me to settle down. I was ready but I was just as content playing the field. It was Baltimore. A lot of the wholesome women were taken and frankly, those types were boring. Wasn't no bitch about to bore me to death. That was probably my problem. What I wanted wasn't good for me. I was no good guy, but I still had a thing for bad girls and broads I had no business dealing with.

At the thought of what I wanted, I glanced down at my phone. I had missed calls from two of my hoes and several text messages from a few others. Some one-nightstands and some were on-again-off-again link ups. None were ever consistent.

After Chelsea, I didn't let bitches get that close to

me. My thoughts drifted to Easton. Now she was one that didn't cause me to shudder at the thought of lingering in my presence. She was fuckable for sure, but something deep inside of me told me that she wasn't like anyone I'd ever ran across. Something also told me that she wouldn't bore me either. She was carrying something, and I wasn't sure if it was nosiness or genuine concern that intrigued me.

She had a husband; yet the few times I was near her, I felt a vibration. A connection. A happily married woman would stay away from a man like me. From the moment I saw her again, seated at the booth with her people, I declared her my quiet mission. I'd given her that look. That I was interested. I'd seen it in her eyes, that she knew. I was a player by birth, so my actions were subtle. To see what she would allow. She'd allowed me to take her home that night instead of calling and waiting on her husband. That was all I needed. Getting in that pretty, little head and body would be one of my new priorities. Finding out who she was. What she stood for. Operation Easton.

~

I had a love and hate relationship with the Baltimore Money Mob. B double M or BMM. My daddy was the leader and founder of it, so it was only right that my brother and I would take over if anything ever happened to him or when he got old. The problem was it happened a lot sooner than everyone planned for. When it was time to pass his crown, we weren't young enough to be put in position. Juanita Garcia McCarter was our mother. Wife to Edward McCarter, aka E Money. My father.

My pops controlled most of the dope movement in West and East Baltimore. When he got locked up after his homie ratted him out for a couple of bodies, the niggas pushing weight on a similar level were scurrying the streets like roaches to take over his territory. Instead of losing money, as well as his reign on the street, my father decided to crown someone else so that business wouldn't be affected. The problem was there were no men to crown. The only people he could trust were women. My mother and my auntie. His younger brother was deceased, killed in a drug deal gone bad, and his closest homie had just sold him out to the police for a sentence reduction. My mother and my auntie were the only feasible options if he wanted to remain in charge. With that said, he crowned them both and together they continued my father's drug enterprise.

Resentment. That's what I felt for my father. I never believed that the drug game was a place for women. He knew that too but his greed and desire to remain on top outweighed his common sense and beliefs. Women were biologically inferior. Given to man to be protected. Not to be preyed upon. Niggas that were being led by the infamous E Money, now being forced to fall in line for females. Several members of the crew had no problem expressing their disdain for his decision. But he didn't care. What he said was law. It had always been that and would always be that. Or so he thought. My mother and auntie led the BMM for six months before our entire family was ambushed. I remembered it like it was yesterday.

"Come on, Ma. Just one more game," I begged, gripping the controller tighter.

"I said no!" she snapped, striding across the room with that authority only she had. "Bed. Now. We gotta be up early to see your father."

Before I could plead my case, she yanked the cord from the wall. The TV screen went black, the game over in an instant.

"Damn, Ma!" Kobra groaned from beside me, but her glare shut him up quick.

"Watch your mouth. And if you keep whining, you won't be opening a single gift tomorrow. Matter of fact, I'll make you wait 'til New Year's."

That threat was all it took. Me and Kobra shuffled toward our beds, mumbling under our breaths. It was Christmas Eve. As much as I wanted to play the game, I wasn't about to mess up my shot at tearing into those boxes under the tree. Our Christmas mornings always hit different—gifts stacked high, food for days, and Ma humming old-school R&B in the kitchen like she was a black woman instead of a Latina.

I slid under the covers and felt her soft kiss on my forehead. She then walked over and did the same to Kobra. "Buenas noches, mis hijos," she whispered, her Puerto Rican accent wrapping around the words like a warm blanket.

"Goodnight, Ma," I muttered, already feeling the buzz of excitement building.

Sleep was hardly in our plans. Me and Kobra stayed up, whispering about what could be waiting for us in the morning. Who got the most gifts? How happy would our dad be when he saw us at the visit? Our voices were low, but the energy between us was electric.

Then the gunshot came.

This was no firecracker or random pop from the block. This one was sharp, loud, definitive. It froze me in place, my chest tightening like someone had their hands around my throat.

Then came the yelling—high-pitched and frantic. Shuffling. Footsteps. Another shot.

I sat up, heart pounding so loud it drowned out my thoughts. Ma always said I had my daddy's name but not his blood. I wasn't built for this. Twelve years old, still sneaking his dirty mags and stuffing my face with cereal like a regular kid. I wasn't ready to protect nothing.

But I knew.

Before I even opened the door, I knew. The way the house felt—cold, heavy.

"Ma?" My voice cracked, barely above a whisper.

Kobra was across from me in his bed, wide-eyed and frozen. Then came the footsteps, heavy and deliberate, climbing the stairs.

The door slammed open, and there he was. Someone unrecognizable. Mask, gloves, nameless.

Boom! The explosion of pain was so fast I didn't even

know where it hit me. My body jerked back, hot tears blinding me. Another shot.

"Kobra!" I screamed, or maybe I didn't. The silence swallowed everything—my brother's voice, my heartbeat, my whole world.

I couldn't move. Couldn't scream. All I could do was lie there, the metallic taste of blood in my mouth, and wait for whatever was coming next.

That day would haunt me forever.

I was shot in the face with the bullet going through my cheek and making a clean exit out the other side. That's where I got my scar from. Kobra was shot in the head. Thankfully, we survived. Unfortunately, we would both be left with eternal scars. Kobra now took Keppra to treat seizures caused from Traumatic Brain Injury and I probably had PTSD or some shit. That night would also eventually be the reason I went to prison.

My brother and I were twelve when our mother died. My auntie accidently revealed the name of her killer to me when I was eighteen. I was never supposed to know. My father's decision of course. It was someone who he'd trusted. Someone who would ultimately cross him. For the second time, my father's major flaw was revealed. He was a bad judge of character and had poor decision-making skills. It had destroyed his family. I didn't tell Kobra that I knew until after I'd laid the motherfuckers down. We'd changed but because of the injuries he'd sustained, he never became as vicious as I had become. He was a menace, but I was a motherfuckin' monster. Kobra could regulate and lead, but he wasn't a thinker like I was. That was the reason he remained second in command while I was away.

I was openly rebellious, but for whatever reason, my father respected me. He felt that I could run an empire despite my sometimes-blatant opposition to authority. For that reason, he removed the crown from my auntie and placed it on my head when I got released from prison at the age of twenty-eight. At times, I openly challenged my father's decisions and leadership; yet he kept me in charge. In his eyes, I was the best choice because the streets had gotten much more dangerous. Much more vicious. And he needed someone vicious as the lead of BMM. All because he yearned to retain his title of king. I didn't respect him, and he couldn't control me. And for that reason, my father was truly the enemy. When a man wanted to be in control, he would do anything. And one thing I would never do is slip up and be too trusting like he was. Even if he was my pops. For that reason, I ruled with an iron-fist and the only nigga I trusted in Baltimore Money Mob, was Kobra.

"I'm gonna keep this shit short and sweet. Prices finna go up."

I was standing in front of the entire gang in a body shop owned by a BMM member named Loco. Kobra and him were close and while I didn't trust him, I trusted Kobra. If he said he was thorough, then I believed it. We usually met in The Blu Bar office, but after the police had been all through the building, I no longer trusted meeting there. Shit could be bugged.

The sound of groaning filled the air before a bunch of chattering erupted after news of a price increase.

"The fuck going on? It's a drought or something. Some shit going on that we not hip to yet?" a nigga name Cato asked.

"Something like that," Kobra replied coolly. "Main thing is we're on the radar now and we weren't before."

The whole gang knew what was up, but no one spoke on it. Benny was what was going on. He wasn't present because the police had picked him up and questioned him earlier that day. He had been told to stay away until further notice.

"For the reasons previously mentioned, we're decreasing our product so we can focus on minimizing slip ups. Y'all gon' eat the cost," Kobra continued.

More groans. I waited until they stopped to explain why.

"When you BMM you operate with a certain level of integrity. When you see other mafuckas aren't, you should be checking them and then informing the right people."

"I ain't no snitch," someone called out.

I didn't even bother to ask or check to see who made the statement.

"It ain't snitching when you call a mafucka out on his shit. To his face, in front of everyone."

The room got quiet with a few people nodding in agreement.

"There's a lot of you niggas that's abusing your BMM membership. I know we all in this together to cop whatever we want. Whether it's a house, a car, or a bitch. Take vacations or whatever," I said.

"But there's no reason why a nigga should think for a second that he can come in a place we own and move crazy. Nobody's above the team. Nobody's above the money," Kobra continued.

It was important that we drilled that shit in their heads because if we didn't, everybody was going to start acting out. Benny had been on bullshit. I'd heard rumors but I didn't know it was that bad. Egypt wasn't the first side piece he'd beat up. He'd beaten up a few before her. Had knocked out one's tooth. Had given another permanent eye damage. A month before he'd shot at a nigga that tried to run off on him, which was understandable, and he'd assaulted several civilians. It was part of the gang life we lived, but what he failed to do was keep us abreast of everything that occurred. If a nigga ran off with some BMM shit and one of our members decided to blow his top off, Kobra and I should be the first to know before his brain fragments had the chance to dry on the ground. Benny wasn't doing none of that. He was doing what he wanted and running around like he was the one in control. Niggas knew but they said nothing. That made them all responsible.

Benny wasn't the only one out of control. There had been rumors of niggas cutting the product down and even copping from other teams. I had to re-shift my focus to get respect re-established. I wasn't for keeping niggas around who didn't move right. You either moved with integrity, got the fuck on, or got laid down. It was that simple.

"Y'all got any questions?" I asked, not really giving a fuck if they did or didn't. "The price increase takes effect immediately. When you pick up ya shipments tomorrow, make sure you have that extra cash. Kobra will keep you posted on the numbers."

Everyone nodded.

"Y'all free to leave."

Everyone left the building and after a few minutes Kobra and I went behind them. We were about to have a conversation that was only for our ears.

❧

I had business to tend to but the only thing I could fucking think about was a bitch. Easton's big, fine, sexy, red ass sat at the forefront of my thoughts while I was supposed to be figuring out all the shit I had going on. I'd found out the name of the nigga whose ass I beat at my baby mama's crib. His name was Lonnie, and after our run in, he called himself putting word out that he wanted smoke.

I was a boss so he already knew I couldn't be easily touched. Because of this, his whole crew EMB, or East Side Mob Boys had declared war on BMM. They had no wins but unfortunately it was going to be a lot of blood shed before those stupid motherfuckers realized that. I hoped to put an end to the shit before it even started. I had enough shit going on because of Benny. The last thing I needed was a mini war. Especially behind some shit that I had started.

"Ten thousand on him. Triple if it's done by tomorrow."

That was the order I'd put out. I'd been raised to give zero fucks about life. The only ones that mattered were the ones we loved. Any others could be flicked off the face of the earth. My goal was to take Lonnie out fast and let every nigga on the East Side know that we didn't fuck around over West. Lonnie was officially a dead man walking. If they decided to retaliate for his death, then I was gonna start taking out the heads.

Kobra, my twin, was my right-hand man. Born an hour apart, I was the older brother. He was just as business savvy and ruthless as I was. The restaurant and bar had been his idea. He was also the reason we had nearly tripled in size in a few years. Solely responsible for the expansion. He was smart, ruthless, and highly capable, but because of his traumatic brain injury, my pops and aunt weren't comfortable letting him take the reins the way I would have liked for him to.

Flashing bright lights, loud noises, and too much stimulation could all trigger an episode for Kobra. That was the reason we went with a still blue hue in the club, rather than flashing lights. It was the reason why the music didn't go past a certain octave.

It was eight in the morning and I had just dropped my daughter off to school. I'd been staying at the big house, so her school wasn't far. Being with my daughter daily was a brutal reminder that it was time for me to settle down. At her age, she required a lot. She was busy, liked to play, needed help with homework, and relied on an adult to make sure she ate and bathed. Aunt Kim had been helping out but after a week had passed, she started to get on my ass about being responsible.

'I didn't help raise no bitch nigga,' were her exact words. To keep it real, I was kind of overwhelmed. I had a crooked detective on my payroll that was keeping me posted on everything that was going on with Benny. They'd asked him about his affiliation with the owners of The Blu Bar as well if we were tied to any drug distribution. That quickly, an assault case at a club had become an investigation against me and my brother. They were snooping and felt they had something and that wasn't good.

I was the boss. I was supposed to have everything under control, but I didn't feel like I did. I could've killed Benny but as much as I disliked his ass, I didn't want to do that because he was BMM. I didn't want to lead with fear. I wanted to be respected. Killing one of our own could make them feel like they were all disposable. That could lead to problems. I wanted to appear just and fair. I wasn't sure what to do and for the first time in a long time, I was going to have to go to my auntie, or worse, my pops.

I walked through the door of The Hair Bistro and was greeted by a half dozen female faces staring me down in blatant satisfaction. The place looked the same as the last time I was there, only it was much more crowded. I scanned the faces and finally found the one I was searching for. Easton was stationed in the corner. While all the stylists gave me lustful stares, she stood there with her face turned up like she wasn't happy to see a nigga. I liked that about her. The fact that she gave me attitude. Most bitches would bow at a nigga feet, but she wasn't for it. She'd practically cursed me out the first time we met, and the encounter still stuck with me. My mama had been firm and so was my auntie. Her delivery reminded me so much of theirs. I could tell she could be loving, but she was also stern. A nigga like me needed those type of women in my life.

I tossed my head back in a quick nod to acknowledge everyone and then walked straight to the corner where Easton was prepping hair and putting it on a rack with spikes sticking off.

"Wassup E," I greeted her with a smile. My eyes wandered her frame openly in satisfaction. Top to bottom. Bottom to top. She was perfect. Even through her black stylist smock, I could see her hips protruding from it.

"Kyson," she said, her tone flat.

There was no smile, but the rise and fall of her chest

told me what I needed to know. I could sense her excitement. Her nervousness. She tried to play it off, but she was excited. Her eye contact, her blank expression. All intentional. I understood why. She wasn't supposed to be interested. She had a man, and she was trying to stop something before it started. Playing tough was her way of doing that. It reminded me of my adolescent days. There was always that girl that liked a nigga but would be mean as fuck.

"How you been?" I asked, standing in front of her station.

She frowned in confusion while her girlfriend that was with her the last two times that I saw her, shot her curious looks.

"You coming to me like we're friends or something. Like that's a question you have the right to ask me."

I smirked. She was showing out in front of everyone that was in the shop now. I could tell she cared about what others thought of her.

"Yeah, well I may have gotten a little ahead of myself. We not there yet, but we will be," I said confidently.

Easton stopped pulling hair from the bundle she was holding and set it down.

"If you want to make an appointment for your daughter. She pointed to her girlfriend. "Tyra will be happy to send you the information."

She grabbed her purse and keys off her station.

"I'm gonna run to the store," she told Tyra. She then looked around. "Anyone want anything?"

All the girls shook their head, so she headed toward the door.

"Have a good day sir," she turned around and said to me before she exited the shop.

A few of the girls quietly snickered, but I didn't give a fuck. She'd tried to play me, but I was still that nigga. The shit was kind of confusing since she'd hugged me and we seemed cool after I took her home.

I looked over at Tyra and her chair was empty. A thought came to my mind and I figured I could use that to my advantage.

"Can you take a nigga as a walk-in?" I asked her.

"*I can*," one of the thirsty bitches offered.

"Thanks shorty, but I want her." I pointed at Tyra.

"Yeah. Sure," Tyra quickly replied, waving me over. "I don't have anyone else coming in for at least another hour. What are you trying to get?" she asked.

"Just a take down," I told her.

I could've taken down my own braids but I wanted to get in sis' chair so I could pick her brain about her friend. I had a feeling that for the right price, she would tell me what I needed to know.

"Have a seat," Tyra said.

I sat down and she snapped open a cape, placed it over me and secured it at the nape of my neck.

She began removing the rubber bands at the ends of my braids and when she was done, she began to quickly unravel them using a comb.

"So, you like Easton?" she asked, cutting to the chase.

My lips curled into a grin. I liked that she didn't bullshit.

"Like? Uhhhhh. More like I'm intrigued by her."

"Same thing."

"She married though."

It was a statement, but it still sounded like a question. I looked around the shop. We weren't loud but I didn't want everybody all up in our conversation. They didn't seem to be paying us any mind; yet I still chose to remain selective with my words.

"She is married. She's been through a lot and I won't speak on what they got going on. What I will say is, if you intend to pursue her, have good intention. She's fragile and deserves happiness. If you're not coming with that, move around."

I let her words sink in. She hadn't said much but she'd said a lot at the same time. I could tell they were close and the fact that she hadn't shut me down told me that her marriage was some bullshit.

"She told me to get at you about a booking site. I want to schedule my daughter for an appointment," I half lied.

"I can text you the link to her booking site."

"She ain't got a card or something?" I asked.

Before she could reply, my phone began to ring.

I looked down. Ciara. She had a big ass and mediocre pussy, so I didn't feel like talking to, let alone entertaining her. I actually no longer felt like entertaining anybody. Not anybody old anyway. I pressed ignore and continued my conversation. Less than ten seconds later, my phone rang again.

"What the fuck?" I murmured.

I looked down. This time it was Caleb. He was with the gang, so I answered.

"Yo," I greeted him.

"Done mission. But with issues."

"Okay. I'll see about it later. I'm busy."

"Hit me when you ready to hear," he said before abruptly disconnecting the call.

I cursed internally. *What the fuck could have gone wrong?* My phone rang again. This time I excused myself. I got up from the chair and walked outside to take the call. It was Chelsea. I had a feeling her call was related to the one that I'd just gotten from Caleb.

"Yo."

"You fucking piece of shit! I know it was you! You killed!"

I didn't even let the bitch finish. I hung up the phone and straight blocked her. I still wasn't sure what was going on but I damn sure wasn't about to let her blow down my line with a bunch of incriminating texts or calls. Besides, she was on ten, screaming and shit in the phone, and I wasn't about to listen to all that noise either.

I stuffed my phone back in my pocket and returned inside. When I got to the chair, Tyra was handing me a card and my phone was ringing again. I didn't bother to pull it out. I figured it was probably Kobra. As the underboss, he'd probably gotten the same call from

Caleb. I looked down at the card Tyra had handed me. *Easton Blue. Hairstylist.*

"I gotta go so you don't gotta worry about taking the rest of my shit out," I told her.

Before she could reply, I pulled out a one-hundred-dollar bill and handed it to her. After she took it, I pulled off five more but held them steady in my hand.

"How about I go ahead and take your number. So, I can get with you about sis."

Tyra hesitated.

"I see how you looking but you should want what's best for your people. Do that … and put a few dollars in your pocket," I encouraged.

She stared me down and then smirked.

"Easton's my best friend. Put your money in your pocket." She turned around and grabbed her own personal card off her station. "My cell is on there. When you hit me up, make sure you come correct," she said smugly.

I took the card and replied. "Trust me, I will.

~

The hum of the Lamborghini Urus filled the quiet Baltimore streets as I cruised toward the Inner Harbor. The leather wheel felt smooth under my palms, a reminder of what six short years in the game and my father's legacy had earned me. The city might've looked peaceful from this angle, but I knew better. Baltimore was a jungle, and I was king of it.

I was on my way to Loco's body shop. It wasn't even noon and already the day had been long. After leaving the hair salon, I called Kobra on a secure line and was informed that the hit I'd put on Lonnie had resulted in him being injured and his sister being killed. She was fifteen. It took everything out of me not to flip the fuck out. A kid! A fucking kid. My team was getting sloppier and sloppier by the day and I took full responsibility for it. It started at the head. Benny had put us in a hole, but I'd just dug the bitch deeper.

The flick of blue and red lights in my rearview pulled me out of my thoughts.

"The fuck?" I muttered, slowing down on Martin Luther King Jr. Boulevard. A cop car. Two, actually.

Despite it being in the middle of the day, the traffic was luckily thin, enabling me to easily pull over. I let the Urus roll to a stop by the curb while sighing in annoyance. As if I didn't have enough shit going on. I couldn't help but wonder what they'd pulled me over for. I wasn't speeding and I didn't remember breaking any traffic laws. I reached in my console and pulled out my information. I wanted them to make this shit quick.

The officer tapped on my window, flashlight shining in my face. I rolled it down slowly, refusing to show any drop of emotion. The cops fed off fear and I wasn't about to give them motherfuckers the satisfaction.

"Problem, officer?"

"License and registration," he said, his tone icy.

I handed it over, staying silent. I wasn't giving them

more than they needed. My face was calm, unreadable. My eyes scanned my passenger rearview mirror. I was already clocking his partner, who was circling the car like I had something to hide.

"You in a rush somewhere, Mr. McCarter?" the first cop asked, eyeing my driver's license.

"If I were in a rush, I would be speeding. Which you saw for yourself, I wasn't," I replied. I didn't have time for pleasantries.

"Step out of the vehicle," he said, stepping back.

I sighed dramatically. "I see y'all ready to waste a nigga time. Is this really necessary?"

I was becoming agitated. The cops hadn't bothered me the past six years I'd been out. All they knew was that I went into prison a kid and came out a law-abiding citizen despite being the son of a gang leader. I knew they watched, but up until recently, they had no reason to fuck with me. Within a week, that had changed.

"Step out," he repeated, hand already hovering near his holster like I was a threat. His partner stood by. He was young. Quiet. Probably a rookie.

I climbed out slow, and deliberate. Pedestrians walked by, while some of them stopped to look at the exchange. I didn't give a fuck. I had nothing to be ashamed nor embarrassed about. They didn't have shit and I wasn't saying shit.

∽

*T*he station was colder than usual. Much colder than the last time I'd been in there. They'd shoved me into a small room with a metal table and chairs bolted to the floor, a single light overhead making my experience feel like a scene out of some cheap cop show. I leaned back in the chair, legs stretched out, arms crossed. My lawyer, Andrew, was already at my side, calm and collected like always.

Across from us sat two detectives: Bradley, who looked like he drank on the job, and Wilson, a skinny motherfucker who thought he was smarter than he really was.

Wilson started first. "From what we're being told, you've been busy, haven't you, Kyson?"

I didn't answer, just stared at him, my face blank. I let him talk. They loved to hear themselves. They also loved to lie, but I of course wasn't falling for none of that shit.

"Lonnie Phillips," Wilson continued. "Ring a bell? Or maybe his sister, Lana? Apparently, you put a hit out on Lonnie, but Lana was the one who ended up dead. Word is, you had something to do with that."

Andrew leaned forward, cutting him off. "My client isn't here to entertain your baseless theories. Either charge him or let him go."

Bradley smirked. "Oh, we're not done. There's also the little situation that happened at The Blu Bar. Nice spot, by the way. Real upscale. Shame the public will soon know that it was funded and probably still being funded by members of the Baltimore Money Mob. Hence the reason that ya boy Benny was able to beat up a woman and pull out a firearm and try to shoot a guy that tried to stop him without any consequences. Care to comment?"

I leaned forward then, resting my elbows on the table. My voice was calm, measured. "Suck my dick."

Bradley's smirk faltered, but Wilson wasn't done. "We've got a white guy who identified Benny. Says Benny was beating on some girl, and when he tried to step in, Benny pulled out his gun and assaulted him. They got to tussling and Benny opened fire in your club. Funny how there's no surveillance or video recording of the incident in a popular spot like The Blu Bar. You make millions of dollars off that place. You mean to tell me you don't have cameras that function correctly?"

I stared at him for a long moment before shaking my head, slow and deliberate. "Nah."

Andrew cut in again. "Unless you have evidence tying my client directly to any crime, we're done here."

Bradley leaned back, clearly annoyed. "You think you're untouchable, McCarter, but remember … everyone can be brought down. Ask E-Money."

I gave him a cold smile. "I'm nothing like that nigga," I said before being led out by my lawyer.

~

*T*he cold October air hit me as I stepped out of the precinct, Andrew trailing behind. The temperature had dropped over the course of several hours. That was how long those fuck ass cops had tied me up. I was headed to pick my daughter up from school. I would be a little late but at least I would be there.

While I blew in my hands and headed to my car, Andrew kept talking about how we were going to "handle things", moving forward. I'd already tuned him out. My mind was elsewhere—on Chelsea, on Benny, on how shit was just lovely but now fucked all up. I had to make some changes. Not just to stay out of prison, but also to ensure my daughter had some stability. She needed her father and a sense of normalcy. I sure as fuck wasn't banking on her mother to ensure that.

I climbed into the Urus, shutting the door on Andrew's voice. My phone was already in my hand before I even pulled out of the lot.

The line rang twice before Kobra picked up.

"Yo," he said, his tone sharp and clipped like always.

"We've got a problem," I said, cutting straight to it. "If you're not already there, I'll see you at the big house."

"Say less," Kobra said, and the line went dead.

KIMBERLY MCCARTER

The vibration of my phone caused my eyes to shift from the stove to the countertop where it lay. I wiped my hands on a nearby dish towel and walked over to it to pick it up. I stopped when I saw that it was my brother calling from Jessup Correctional Institution. Edward McCarter aka E-Money McCarter was Kyson and Kobra's father. He along with our late brother Eli were legends in the street. I should've been one too but being a female, my prominent role would always be secret, and my contribution undervalued.

I'd always resented the game for not taking women seriously, but I was to the point now that I was used to it. I still commanded respect and called shots niggas never knew about. I loved both my brothers dearly growing up but as I got older, my feeling of resentment would replace that of love. Especially for E-Money.

"You not gon' answer that?"

I had returned to the stove, but Kobra's voice caused me to turn around.

"No. It's your father. He doesn't want shit, and he's just gonna say the same thing. "Have Kyson come see me." I mocked my brother's voice. "We know he won't. Not until he's good and ready."

E didn't want shit but to bark orders and pretend to still be in control. He hadn't been in control for the last sixteen years. Ever since Kyson learned who killed his mother and shot the three of us, E had lost control. Kyson resented him just like I did. But for different reasons.

The Baltimore Money Mob was our family business, and long before Kyson and Kobra came into the world, it was run by family. That was until Juanita showed up with her charm, wit, and promises to make us even more money. My brother overlooked a lot of shit when it came to the people he cared for. Juanita wasn't the woman she claimed to be, and E-Money knew it; yet he ignored her ways because she was the pipeline to his connect. The pipeline to the Hispanic drug market. I'd always told him and Eli that we could do without it. But as always, E put his wants over everything.

"What about Kyson?" Kyson asked, walking into the kitchen where Kobra sat and I continued to stand over the stovetop.

"Your father was calling. I was just saying he's gonna ask me to tell you to call him. Where's Zoe?" I asked.

"She's in her room, watching cartoons."

I smiled. The thought of Zoe being there with us for good warmed my heart. I was all about family and was the type of person who didn't mind several generations living under one roof. That was the reason I'd convinced Kyson to purchase the house. Seven bedrooms with six bathrooms, there was plenty of space for a few more children and Kobra and Kyson's wives. Whenever they decided to stop playing around and start living for the shit that truly mattered.

I always told them that they were getting too old to be slinging dick. They were thirty-four years old, just shy of thirty-five. As grown as they were, their selection of women worried me. The boys wanted to be the total opposite of their father; yet they were so much like him it scared me. They liked bad girls. Women who were edgy and although at times good people, brought baggage with them. Women like their mama.

"Well, dinner will be ready soon. Chicken and gravy, broccolini and mashed potatoes."

"Sounds good," Kobra said unenthusiastically.

That was unlike him. While him and Kyson were identical, their appetites certainly weren't. Kobra was the twin that would eat the leftovers, lick the icing bowl clean, and wipe out the refrigerator.

"What's going on?" I turned around and asked.

Something was up. The energy was off, and I knew those two motherfuckers like I knew myself. They knew when I asked that question that they'd better give it to me straight.

"I got taken in for questioning by the cops," Kyson replied.

"For?"

"The shit with Benny at the club."

He paused but I could detect the hesitation in his eyes.

"And?" I had a feeling there was more.

"The shit with the nigga Lonnie at Chelsea's house. I put a hit out on him because he basically vowed retaliation against me. The hit went wrong, and his fifteen-year-old sister was killed."

"Fuck Kyson!" I yelled, slamming my fist on the kitchen counter, accidently knocking over the stirring spoon in the process.

"Keep your voice down Auntie," Kyson replied, looking back towards the living room where Zoe's bedroom was close by.

"Shut the fuck up," I said harshly. "Your stupid ass wanted to prove a point so bad and didn't prove shit. Benny's shit is one thing, but this is your fault. Fix it. And fix it fast."

"That's what we're trying to do," Kobra replied in a voice that seemed a little too irritated for me. I didn't play with either of them. Their mama was no longer here, and, in a sense, I was their mama.

"Kobra ... Unless you want to get smacked, I suggest you shut up."

"What do you suggest?" Kyson asked.

I looked at him with the same look I always gave his father. While the boys respected my opinion, E only respected it when shit had become dire. We were all strategic thinkers, but I was the most calculating. Even when Kyson was away, Kobra was the face while I was the shadow. BMM may have looked at Kyson like he was the king, but he was truly a prince because I was the queen. I ran shit and made the final calls when difficult decisions had to be made.

"I suggest you stop getting in your feelings about these whores and find someone to settle down with first and foremost. Second, you both are gonna chill for now. Maybe a week or two. I'll handle Benny."

"And how do you plan to do that?" Kyson asked.

"Benny should've been put down right after he pulled that pistol in The Blu Bar. You know what I plan to do."

I left it at that. E-Money was ruthless. So were Kobra and Kyson. But I was Kimberly McCarter. The most ruthless of them all.

"I'll take care of this Lonnie situation."

"Keep Chelsea out of it. She is still the mother of my child." Kyson said before getting up and walking out of the kitchen.

"I'd hardly call that bitch a mother. But I'll do my best," I told him.

EASTON BLUE

"Hey boo!" Wave sang as she walked into the shop carrying the Chinese food that I'd requested nearly an hour ago. She was just in time because I was starving. It was nearly six in the evening and I hadn't eaten all day.

"What I tell you about coming in here making all that noise," Tyra asked her with a playful frown.

She ran a flat iron through her client's freshly installed weave while she eyed Wave.

"Girl please. As many times as I've heard yo' big mouth from outside on the street. And stop acting like you own the place," Wave shot back. She returned Tyra's playful frown with her own before plopping down behind the receptionist desk.

"Where's Ky at?" Wave asked as if she would magically appear in the shop.

"With her grandma," I replied. "Where else?"

I had one more head to do so while I waited, I got a

head start prepping hair for tomorrow on my rack but stopped so I could go eat my food.

"Girl, when are you going to enroll her in school, and don't that old lady get tired of listening to and running behind kids all day?" she asked.

"I'm still looking for a good preschool. You know my baby ain't going to no public school. And her grandmother never gets tired of her," I assured her. "They love my baby over there and I only work three days a week. It's not like she has her every single day."

"Well, it sure seems that way. Every time I call or drop in, I don't ever see her. Ain't that lady married? Couldn't be me. I'd rather be getting my back blown out from dick than running behind somebody else's bebe kids."

She laughed while tearing open the plastic bag holding two orders of four wings fried hard with salt, pepper and ketchup.

"Bitch my child ain't bad. Now Zalo's sister Pita … Her kids are bad. They a whole different breed. Pita don't seem to mind though because she keeps having em."

Pita was one of those young girls who was too fertile for her own good. Every other year she'd spit out a kid. She was on baby number three. Two different baby daddies and far as hell away from being married.

It irritated my soul that Zalo took care of her and their kids, as well as their mother. He made hella money in the drug game but couldn't even completely enjoy and spend it the way he wanted to because he was too busy taking care of his family. It was something I admired in the beginning, but now resented.

"She definitely spit them mafuckas out like she ain't got nothing better to do. What's this? Baby number four?" she asked.

Before I could tell her 'three', the door chimed and when I looked up it was Kyson. He looked comfortable in an Amiri sweater and black distressed jeans. On his neck was a diamond Cuban link necklace. It was simple but at the same time, the sparkle from it was extravagant.

"How y'all ladies doing?" Kyson asked with a big, bright ass smile stretching across his face.

There it was. The tiny gap his brother had mentioned that day at The Blue Bar. It was hardly noticeable but lately I'd been noticing everything. The man was undeniably fine. A lush, wet lip, pretty boy thug. His braids were gone from the day before, and his hair was now pulled to the top of his head in a ponytail.

My thoughts instantly turned dirty. It was something about him that I couldn't put my finger on. He annoyed me but he also entertained me. *Get it together Easton. You're married.* I inhaled and exhaled quietly to rid myself of the butterflies that had formed in my stomach.

"You not gon' say good morning?" Kyson asked, looking surprised after everyone spoke but me.

"No."

"I thought we were cool. We were just fine the other night."

My face flushed red from embarrassment. It was clear as day on my light skin. The way he said it, made it seem like we had done something we weren't supposed to be doing. Luckily, it was only four of us in the shop, not including him. Me, Wave, Tyra, and another stylist name Ginger. She was packing up to leave. Everyone had heard his statement, but I still chose to ignore it instead of addressing it.

This was the second day in a row that he had stopped in seemingly to see me. It wasn't a good look, but I'd be a lie if I said I minded.

Kyson shook his head in amusement watching my face.

"You know ... You're a little ungrateful."

"Ungrateful?" I asked. That I couldn't ignore.

"Did I stutter?"

I looked around the shop after his remark.

"You know what. You can get out being ignorant." I was serious, but the message came out playful instead of hostile.

"Ignorant means lacking knowledge or understanding. You want me to get out for being honest or in your opinion rude? If rude is what you meant, you're actually the rude one. I went out of my way for you and showed you kindness; yet I haven't gotten that in return. I'm also a customer. I have an appointment set with you for six; yet I couldn't even get a hello."

"You're my six-o clock?" I asked in surprise as I crunched down on my chicken.

"Yeah," he chuckled.

"You booked for stitch braids?"

He nodded.

"Shit I'm sorry."

"Don't be sorry. Be better. And why you so mean? You too pretty to be acting so thugged out."

I continued chewing while Wave sat quietly, watching our interaction.

"Well, when you've been through some of the shit, I've been through, you'd be a little rough too." I told him.

"Bye y'all. I'll see everyone tomorrow," Ginger called out, right before exiting the shop.

I noticed Tyra's client getting up and handing her money while she rushed around cleaning up. My bestie was moving like she had somewhere to be.

"You leaving?" I asked while watching her stuff her money in her smock and continue sweeping up her station.

"Yeah. I'm done for the day. I told you about leaving your books open like that for last minute appointments."

She looked at Kyson.

"No offense." She forced a smile.

"None taken," he said.

"He won't take long at all. I'll be out by six-thirty, seven latest." I looked at him. "You can have a seat in my chair. Give me five minutes. I'm gonna eat some of this food real quick and then I'll get started."

Kyson nodded and headed over to my station while Tyra grabbed her purse and keys and walked over to the receptionist desk where Wave and I were sitting.

"One of y'all let me get a wing," she asked.

"Now you know not to ask me. As much shit as you talk to me," Wave replied, looking at Tyra like she'd lost her mind. "Plus, I'm about to go. I gotta be to work at seven so I'm going to eat the rest of my shit later."

"Selfish, greedy ass," Tyra mumbled as she rolled her eyes at Wave.

I held my bag out for her to grab a wing. She reached in and quickly pulled one out.

"Thanks best." She immediately bit into it.

"You're welcome bookie. Drive safe and call me when you get in," I told her. I was hoping she had it in her heart to wait for me, but apparently, she didn't.

"Will do. Bye Wave. Bye Kyson," she said, before proceeding to the door. Before she walked out, she turned around and began speaking to Kyson. "You gon' make sure she's good?" she asked him.

"I got her," he said before I could even protest.

"Thank you," she sang, before shooting a grin in my direction and walking out the door.

~

*I*t took me thirty minutes to have Kyson's hair braided. He'd come in already washed and blow-dried thankfully, so he was in and out of my chair in no time. The entire time he was there he tried to make small talk, but I kept it light, answering his questions with 'yes' and 'no' answers. The type of questions he was asking, gave me the impression that he was trying to figure me out.

"You're all done," I said to Kyson.

I'd finished his last braid and was now applying a handful of mousse to his head. When I was all done, I handed him a mirror. He held it up to his face.

"Okay," he gloated. "I see you nice with it," he complimented.

I smiled sheepishly. I looked away when I realized that he hadn't lowered the mirror but now held it, so my face reflected with his.

"We make a beautiful couple," he grinned.

"Yeah, I bet," I said, before walking off.

I immediately began to clean up my station while Kyson rose from his chair, dug in his pocket and handed me two, one-hundred-dollar bills.

"That's not necessary. I already received full payment. It shows you paid in full," I reminded him.

"It's a tip. Take it," he demanded.

I took the money from his hand and stuffed the bills into my pants pocket. This time, I said thank you.

"You're welcome. I'll wait for you while you lock up."

I definitely wouldn't protest to that. Our shop was on Frederick Avenue and it wasn't the worse, but it damn sure wasn't the best either.

I gave Kyson a nod and quickly finished sweeping my area. After dumping all the dirt and hair around my station, I tossed it into the trash, and grabbed my purse and keys. Tyra had already made sure everything was off so there was nothing left to do except hit the light switch and lock the door.

Once we got outside, I headed to my truck and noticed one of my tires was flat. And it wasn't slow leak flat, it was flat as fuck. Like I had ran over a nail or some shit.

"Fuck!" I cursed. I looked behind me to see if Kyson was still close and thankfully, he was. I turned around and began walking back to him.

"Hey umm, do you know how to put on a spare?"

He was just about to get into his Lamborghini but stopped.

"Come on baby. I'm a man. Of course, I know how to put on a spare. You got a flat?" he asked.

"Yeah," I replied.

Him being able to put on a spare instantly attracted me more to him. The last time I had a flat, Zalo had drove out and waited for AAA with me. Kyson wasn't just fine; he was also good with his hands.

"Do you have a spare?" he asked.

"I think so," I replied.

I tucked my arms into one another. It was that time of the year when it got dark early and the weather was starting to lean more towards the colder side. While I stood in the parking lot of the shopping center, my lip trembled slightly from the wind whipping against my bare arms.

"You cold?" Kyson asked, staring down at my arms. Goosebumps peppered my skin.

"A little," I admitted.

"Give me your keys and get in."

He pointed to his truck. I mumbled a 'thanks,' passed him my keys and hopped in his whip. It was already started, and I welcomed the heat when I got inside and sank into the plush leather seats. While I got comfortable, he walked over, popped the trunk and began searching for my spare. After taking a long look in my trunk, he returned.

"You don't have a spare mama. I'll call a tow truck and we can get it over to my boys' shop."

"A tow truck? Can't we just go get a spare?" I asked.

I pointed up the street like I knew for sure there was a tire shop up there. I could've sworn I'd seen one on my route to work before. It was a busy area so there had to be one close by. A tow truck would be all day. I had to pick up Kyllie and I wasn't trying to be tied up for hours.

"We could, but that wouldn't make any sense. We'd have to go get the spare and come back and put it on, when we can just get it towed somewhere, they can put on a new tire. and then you won't have to worry about it again."

He had a point, so I nodded and proceeded to go along with his suggestion.

"I gotchu. You with me for the next hour." He grinned, looking as handsome as ever.

I sat back and relaxed in the seat. That didn't sound too bad.

~

"*H*ow'd you get that mark?" I asked, making small talk as Kyson crept through traffic in his Lambo. It was almost like he was intentionally driving slower than normal.

"Long story," he said, his eyes fixed in front of him. "I'll tell you one night," he said casually.

"*Night?*"

"Yeah." He looked at me and grinned. "As in, *one night* when I got you somewhere laid up, I'll tell you all about it."

"What?" I gave a confused look. I knew what he was insinuating and as bold as it was, his remark didn't anger me. Nevertheless, I had to pretend that it did. I mean ... I was married.

"I don't know what you think this is, or what made you think you could say some shit like that to me, but I have a husband."

"I'm not trying to disrespect you. I'm just saying."

He shrugged as if it was no big deal. He looked at me with an even expression.

'That should be taken as a compliment baby. I don't chase and the fact that I'm prepared to chase you, says a lot."

I rolled my eyes.

"That's not a compliment to me, but okay. Why would chasing a married woman even be in your thoughts?"

"If we keeping it real, I don't give a fuck about yo' nigga. He ain't gon' matter when it's all said and done."

A chill swept through me. It wasn't the type of chill you got when you were scared, it was the type you got when a nigga stirred a fire in you. I didn't know why, but it was something about the way his rude ass popped his shit, that did something to my body. His confidence was sexy.

Bitch get a grip. The last thing you need to do is get caught up with some disrespectful, unhinged ass nigga. I didn't know if he was truly unhinged or not, but the way his attitude and mood fluctuated, I'd bet my last dollar that he was.

"What's his name. Not that it matters."

"Well, if it doesn't matter then you don't need to know it."

He smiled and bent the corner.

"His name is Zalo," I finally said after a moment of silence. "Why? You wanna see how you compare to him?"

"I'll never speak down on another nigga." The smirk

he wore caused me to look at him in confusion. He said it like it was something he knew but wouldn't say, so as not to sound like a hater. I didn't bother replying. "I've heard of him though."

"What made you ask for his name?" My curiosity was winning.

"Just want to know whose wife I'm about to take."

Whose wife I'm about to take. His words rang in my ears and another chill ran through my body. He said it like he was so sure. He almost had me questioning my damn self. *Would he conquer me.* Why was I even asking? That was a question that I should've been able to answer. The truth was, I wasn't sure.

"You hungry?" he asked.

"Fuck," I groaned. In a rush to get Kyson's hair done and get out of the shop, I'd forgotten my order of chicken wings.

"What?" he asked.

"I left my food." I slapped my thigh. "I'll just eat it tomorrow."

"Eww. That shit 'bout to sit out all night."

"I don't give a fuck," I laughed. "I've eaten worse."

"You sound like you down bad." He laughed. "We going to get some food. I'll get you extra for tomorrow. So, you don't fuck around and get sick from eating old shit. I know a little spot that makes really good sandwiches."

"I don't know about us being out together eating like that. Why don't you just stop at Popeyes or something," I suggested.

Baltimore was Zalo's city. A lot of people knew him and could easily place my face. I didn't want to get caught up. Kyson immediately frowned at my fast-food suggestion.

"I don't want that shit," he said, as if it were garbage. "I'm not knocking it because I do fuck with it from time to time, but I don't want that right now. If you worried about someone seeing you, I can assure you it's a safe spot. You don't gotta worry about nobody telling your man they saw you," he assured, practically reading my mind. "Your truck is headed to the shop and they're already waiting on your tire. We can sit down and have a bite to eat, and when they're done, we can shoot over there, and you can be on your way."

"Kyson. Look, I don't know what type of games you're playing but I'm a married woman. I can't be out having a fuckin' meal with you," I said irritably.

Kyson chuckled, completely unfazed by my words and tone.

"I'm good in any hood so that means you are too. Worry less when you're with me. Now sit back and shut up. We going to eat."

I walked into Miguel's Deli and Market on Main Street in Highlandtown, and a wave of nostalgia hit me like a warm embrace. The familiar scent of spices, fresh herbs, and roasted coffee mingled in the air, pulling me back to my childhood. Miguel's had always been more than just a store; it was a cornerstone of the neighborhood, where every shelf told a story of community and culture.

"How you been, Zalo!" Miguel called out with a wide grin, his weathered face lighting up as soon as he saw me. He stood behind the counter, wiping his hands on a stained apron. His voice carried the same warmth it always did—a mix of familiarity and genuine care.

"Pretty good. It's been a while," I replied, nodding as I glanced around. The place hadn't changed much— same vibrant walls, same chatter of neighbors catching up over a cup of coffee.

My daughter tugged at my hand, her small frame

bouncing with curiosity as she took in the quiet but usually bustling scene. I'd brought her along on a last-minute errand for my mother. It was almost nine at night and she had run out of *recao* for her stew, and Miguel's was one of the only places in the city where you could find it.

"Too long," Miguel said, his eyes crinkling as they dropped to my daughter. "Hey little one." He smiled kindly before his eyes lifted back to me. "How's your mother and sister?"

"My mom's good. Sister's still having a bunch of babies," I said, shaking my head with a hint of embarrassment.

Miguel chuckled knowingly. "I heard. What can I get for you today?"

"Recao. Mom's making stew."

"I gotchu. It's over in the corner," he said, pointing toward the glass divider that separated the deli counter from the produce section. Miguel's was designed to be everything for everyone—a deli, a market, and a small café where you could sit down and soak in the vibe of the neighborhood.

I made my way to the produce section, where the faint, earthy aroma of herbs filled the air. As I grabbed a bunch of *recao*, I couldn't help but feel at home. Places like this—places like Miguel's—had a way of making you forget the weight of the world, even if only for a moment.

"How's your wife doing?" I asked as I walked back to the counter. Miguel's wife had battled cancer a few years ago, and the community had rallied around him like family. Asking about her had become second nature.

"She's doing great. Body and mouth strong as ever. That woman knows she'll lay me out all kinds of ways every day," Miguel said with a hearty laugh. But as the laughter faded, his expression shifted, his tone turning more solemn. "I didn't know you and your wife had separated. I saw her. She didn't even remember who I was."

The words hit me like a gut punch, and my forehead wrinkled in confusion. "We're not separated. When did you see her?"

Miguel hesitated, his hands fidgeting with a roll of deli paper. "Today. Maybe an hour ago. She and another fella were here. I thought you two were separated."

My chest tightened, the heat of anger rising under my skin. I forced myself to breathe, keeping my voice calm even as my pulse thundered in my ears. It was funny how I dipped out on Easton before she had actually given me permission, but I never thought about how it made her feel. Just the thought of her even being in the company of another man, did something to me.

"What did he look like?"

"You know E-Money's kid. One of the twins. Kyson. Everyone knows him," Miguel said, his voice quieter now, as if he regretted saying anything at all.

Kyson. The name alone made my blood simmer. I knew exactly who he was—a rich, drug boss who along with his brother, moved through Baltimore like they owned the streets. There were only a handful of dealers that sold large scale weight in the Hispanic community. He was one of, if not *the* biggest.

I clenched my jaw, my grip tightening on the bundle of *recao* in my hand. Miguel watched me cautiously, like he could feel the storm brewing beneath my composed exterior.

"Thanks for letting me know," I said, forcing a smile that didn't reach my eyes. My heart pounded as questions raced through my mind. *What the fuck was Easton doing with Kyson?*

As I paid for the *recao* and stepped out of Miguel's, the cold October air hit me, but it did nothing to cool the fire coursing through me.

EASTON BLUE

"*A* little late for you ain't it?" Zalo's voice seemed to come out of nowhere in the dark room.

It startled me, causing me to jump.

"Shit babe. You scared me."

I palmed my chest and breathed in and out deeply as my heart rate began to adjust.

"Where were you?" he asked.

He was sitting in the accent chair in the corner of our room. No light. No phone. No music. Just being creepy. I hit the light switch and his eyes locked on me. The look on his face made me nervous. Like he was angry. I didn't like seeing Zalo angry. No one did.

"I got a flat," I told him.

He was right. It was very late for me. I usually was out of the shop by seven, and after picking up Kyllie from her grandmother's, home by eight. Tonight, she had come home with Zalo. After grabbing food and waiting on my tire, it was after ten before I was on my way. Of course, somewhere along the way, I had lost track of time eating in the truck and running my mouth with Kyson. He was actually pretty cool to be around. We never ran out of things to talk about once we got started and I had to admit, the night actually ended too soon.

Thoughts of my few hours with Kyson were quickly placed to the back of my mind when I realized Zalo was still staring in my direction with a crazed look in his eyes. It was something about the way he was looking at me that made me uncomfortable. It was like he had laser vision and could see right through me. Had someone seen me and ratted me out? I hadn't technically done anything.

"A flat huh?" He stood up from the accent chair and charged me, grabbing me by my throat.

"What the fuck!" I screamed, my hands flying to his so he could loosen his grip.

"Lie to me again and I'll break your fucking neck!" Zalo roared, tightening his grip.

His face was constricted and menacing. His lips pulled tightly into one another. His eyes. Cold, shiny, and black like marbles.

"I'm not lying! I swear," I choked out.

It had been a long time since Zalo had raised his hands to me. But when he did, it was usually extreme and because of his raging jealousy. It was crazy how he could dish it out, but he couldn't take it.

Still squeezing my throat like a sponge, he pushed me towards the bed, while I gripped and clawed at his hands. He released me by pushing me down onto the mattress.

Zalo's eyes scanned the room and settled on my Chanel bag that I'd dropped on the floor when he rushed me and began choking me. He raced to it and tore it open to retrieve my phone.

"Check it! There's nothing in there. I got a fucking flat. Whoever told you they saw me, saw me with a client!"

Someone had to have told him something. There was no way that he would be acting that way if he thought I had been out late with Tyra or a family member.

"He booked a six-o clock appointment on the site," I continued. "I got a flat on the way out and he gave me a ride while the tow truck took it over to a shop."

"For over three fucking hours E!" he yelled. "Do I look like a goofy ass nigga? Why the fuck you ain't call me? Or ride with the tow truck?"

His eyes blazed angrily into mine as he fired off questions. He still held my phone, scrolling through it. There was nothing there. Kyson didn't have my number and I didn't talk to any other men. If anybody talked shit about Zalo, it was in person or over the phone. Never through text messages. The nigga had a history of digging through a bitch phone. He wasn't going to find anything.

"It was dark Za. I had just walked out, and he was right there. I knew you would be a while." Tears slipped down my face.

He tossed my phone on the bed beside me.

"I'm the nigga you call next time. I handle shit when it pertains to you. I don't give a fuck if it takes an hour for me to get there. Shouldn't no nigga be assisting you. You sneaky as fuck and that type of shit got me really questioning why you won't fuck me. You fucking that nigga?" His chest heaved up and down and his eyes were buck as he waited for a response.

"No! I told you he was a client Zalo."

"You better not, because I swear, if I find out you lying, you gon' die beside that motherfucker."

I wiped away the tears from my face as I trembled from his words. I had no doubt that he meant what he said.

~

*L*ater that night, I stood in the shower, washing the days stress from my body. Not long ago, there were days that I wouldn't even want to bathe. Had no desire to and didn't give a damn how I smelled or looked. I was moving through the grieving process. I knew it. I could feel it. I was indulging more in pleasures that I recently felt guilty about. As much as I missed my son, I rarely went in his room. That's where he was. His ... remains. I hated that word. I planned to bury him one day but for the last year, I hadn't been able to bring myself to do it. Guilt kept me out of there. But tonight, I felt different. The anxiety of being in his room was gone.

I was evolving through my grief. I was still heart-broken, but something was driving me to live again. Something was telling me that I wasn't truly dead inside. That I was indeed still very much alive and deserving. That's what Quan would want. I didn't know if it was the pep talks from Tyra, my sister and my cousin, or if it was from that night at The Blu Bar. When the shooting erupted and I couldn't find Wave, Miracle and Tyra, I was triggered. I had an over-whelming fear that I was about to lose them. Like I had lost Quan. That night was a striking reminder that there was still love inside of me. Still people that loved me and I loved them back.

Kyson had stopped me from losing my mind that night. He had that calming spirit. That take charge mentality. And even if he was under pressure, one would never be able to tell it.

I loved Zalo but he didn't have that calming ability. When the police showed up at my house and told me that my son had been killed in an accident, he was by my side, but I felt like I'd received the news alone. He was in shock just like I was and wasn't sure how to console me right away. He had to take it all in first. He was the one that had called Wave. Wave called Tyra, Miracle and a few other homegirls I was friends with it at the time. They had been my rocks.

Pulling myself out of my thoughts, I finished my shower and dried myself off. After slathering some baby oil gel on my smooth, light brown skin, I emerged from the master bathroom and headed back into the bedroom but stopped when I heard Zalo on the phone.

"It's over Lola. I told you this was no forever thing. I'm working on my marriage and you no longer fit in the equation."

From the corner of the door, I watched through the crack. He was frustrated. His brows had dipped, his forehead was tight, and his face was pulled into a tight scowl. Zalo's emotions were never hidden. Never calm and undetectable like Kyson's.

"Do what the fuck you want," he continued to argue. "You're gonna look stupid and you still ain't stopping nothing. I don't give a fuck what you tell her. She ain't going nowhere. We together so get the fuck over it."

He ended the call. I waited a few seconds before making a little noise and coming out the bathroom.

"You were on the phone?" I asked, softly, walking into the room in a black, silk nightgown.

"Yeah."

"With who?" I quizzed. I wanted to see if he would lie to me.

"Lola," he admitted. "She keeps calling me. I blocked her but she's been calling me private and from random motherfuckers' numbers. Nothing to worry about though. I'll handle her. You said you wanted to move forward and do your part, and I promised to do mine. It's always us."

"Never them," I finished.

Zalo had apologized to me earlier after choking me.

I accepted it and agreed to put forth an effort to restore our marriage. There was a fire growing inside of me for intimacy that I hadn't had since my son died. It was new and had came on suddenly. I wanted to lay my head into the pillow at night and talk away my stress from the day. Relax under the weight of my man's arms. I wanted to be loved on. I was tired of wearing the armor of a wounded woman. I wanted to be soft again. I was tired of carrying the weight of worry and pain.

As much as I was attracted to Kyson, I had taken vows. I was going to work on getting back to where I was with my husband. The problem was, deep down, I wasn't sure if I truly wanted to. Zalo was my comfort come, but Kyson had me feeling like stepping outside of it.

EGYPT TESTAYE

*W*hile I sat in the waiting room of Gynemed Surgical Center in Rosedale, nervous butterflies filled my stomach. It wasn't the fact that I was killing my baby that was causing the flutters. As much fucking as I did, I'd never had an abortion so what I was going through was new to me and I was scared as shit. *Would it hurt? Would everything go as planned.* My thoughts raced as I sat. The place was cold, sterile, uninviting. It made the whole process even more intimidating.

To occupy myself, I pulled my phone out of my purse. I pulled up Instagram, letting my thumb mindlessly scroll while my brain tried to tune out the cold, hospital vibe around me. My feed was full of the usual — memes, couples flexing matching outfits, random motivational quotes. Then I saw it.

"Police identify Baltimore man, Benjamin Edwards, as latest homicide victim. Found dead in dumpster.

I froze, staring at the post. The picture was blurry, showing yellow tape and detectives crowded around a crime scene. Benny.

Before I could fully process it, my phone started buzzing with DM notifications. A few of my close friends had sent me the post, their messages full of exclamation points and shocked emojis. *"Ain't this the dude you was messing with?"* *"Yo, you good??"*

My chest tightened, and I swiped out of the messages, not ready to respond. My heart pounded as I read further down into the caption. The words *"throat slit"* jumping off the screen like a slap.

I swiped left on the post, squinting at the grainy picture of a body bag being loaded into a coroner's van. My stomach flipped in a way that had nothing to do with the baby growing inside me.

Kobra.

I felt it in my chest, deep and certain. He said he'd handle Benny; said he'd make sure Benny didn't bother me. But this? My breath caught as guilt clawed its way up my throat.

Benny wasn't perfect, not by a long shot, but he didn't' deserve to die. Didn't deserve to have his throat slit and left in a fuckin' dumpster.

I blinked hard and leaned back against the stiff plastic chair, my phone shaking in my hand. I didn't ask for that. I didn't want his blood on my hands. But there it was, staining me anyway.

My name was finally called, and I shoved the phone into my purse. My legs felt like jelly as I stood up, moving toward the nurse with a fake confidence I didn't feel. This was supposed to be a fresh start, a clean break. Benny was gone, the baby was about to be gone too, but I felt... stuck.

As I walked down the hallway, the cold sterility of the clinic pressed harder against me. I wanted to cry, scream, something—but what good would that do? What was done was done.

Kobra had kept his promise. Benny would never bother me again. But the cost felt higher than I'd ever imagined.

EASTON BLUE

J'd been having more good days than bad
lately. I'd been getting out more and even
planned to attend a Halloween event that Wave had
begged me to go to. The day had been great. Wave,
along with Miracle and I had eaten lunch at The
Cheesecake Factory at Arundel Mills and were now
searching for costumes at a seasonal store in the mall.

"So, what's up with you and that fine ass nigga from
the restaurant?" Miracle asked. "Have you heard from
him?"

I pretended not to hear her while my sister's messy
ass took it upon herself to answer. At times I didn't
know why I still continued to tell her all my damn
business.

"Ohhhhh. She ain't tell you?" Wave said with a
mischievous smile.

"He keeps popping up at the shop to see Miss
Thang."

Wave cut her eyes at me, knowing she was starting some shit.

"Why you ain't tell me?" Miracle's asked, her brows lifting and eyes lighting up like they always did at the mention of some tea.

"What's there to tell? He been coming by trying to shoot his shot, but I'm married."

"Girl pu-lease!" Wave said, catching me all the way off guard. "Since when did that nigga care about being married. That bitch Lola still posts him damn near every day."

I swallowed the lump that had formed in my throat. I'd heard Zalo tell her that they were through.

"Probably old pictures. She just doing shit now to get under my skin."

"Yeah, that may be the case but at this point, I wouldn't give a damn. Zalo don't got that hoe in check and the fine ass nigga that drive the Lamborghini is ready to suck on that pussy."

I rolled my eyes at my sister's vulgar mouth but at the same time, I couldn't help but smirk.

"I meant to ask you how you liked that stew I brought over that day?" Wave continued as she held up what looked like a hooker costume.

"Yo' whole ass gon' be out," I told her. "And the stew was good. Zalo ate all of his the same day and helped me clear what was left of what was in the crock pot."

Wave put the costume back on the rack, stopped and looked at me with a grin.

"You didn't eat any of his, did you?"

"No. I remembered you said it didn't have tomatoes. You know I want the works."

"Good," she said. "Because that wasn't stew bitch. Not for humans anyway. That was dog food. Pedigree. Country stew to be exact."

My words caught in my throat and before I could mouth a curse word, Miracle and Wave began roaring in laughter and high-fiving each other.

"That motherfucker wanna run around like a dog! He can eat like one."

Anger coursed through my veins and all I could do was walk off. As pissed as I was, I couldn't help but find the shit funny as well.

"Don't be mad sis! You know he still my bro," she cackled with Miracle from the other end of the nearly empty store.

I flipped them the bird and stayed my distance while continuing to shop. I loved my sister but sometimes the shit she did was outrageous. *Who the fuck feed a motherfucker dog food?*

I continued to shop quietly, intentionally keeping my distance from Wave's high-yellow ass to avoid sucker punching her. After looking at a slew of costumes, I was still undecided on what to choose. Noticing the back of the store had a wall and a few more racks of costumes I hadn't viewed yet, I headed that direction.

"Take a picture; it lasts longer," Lola said snidely as my eyes landed on her standing with two of her friends, browsing through the same rack that had no one there a minute ago. I had literally just glimpsed at the bitch and she was trying to play me like I was staring at her.

Wave had already gotten under my skin, and now this bitch miraculously appears out of no where. Wave had been posting to her story for the past couple of hours and I had no doubt that Lola's motionless ass had made it her business to be there so she could be seen. She had three of her homegirls with her but that didn't faze me a bit. I was good.

Nevertheless, my mood shifted instantly—from irritated to sour. Lola stood there in a corset and a fitted skirt that hugged her figure, the high slit on her thigh leaving little to the imagination. In person, she looked even better than her online pictures and videos. Sleek ponytail, flawless skin—she was undeniably beautiful. But her character and attitude made her ugly.

"Girl, ain't nobody worried about you," I snapped. "That glance is all the attention you'll ever get from me. It's sad you want to be acknowledged so bad."

I rolled my eyes at the silly bitches she was with. They were standing there like Lola was the ringleader. That bitch wasn't tough by a long shot. She was an internet gangster, She was going to find out if she kept fucking with me. Where I was from, a chick like her would've had her ass handed to her long ago.

Lola smirked, full of herself. "I don't need your acknowledgment, sweetheart. Trust me, I get plenty of attention from your husband."

The room seemed to tilt. Wave and Miracle crept

up behind me. Wave was already pushing her hair back. I reached back and touched her arm, so she knew to relax. My baby sister was always on go but I had shit under control.

"You're a delusional bitch," I spat, my voice sharp and trembling. It was something about her nerve that was enraging me.

Lola's smirk widened. "Delusional? That's rich, coming from you. Your husband had two kids behind your back, and instead of manning up, he got his sister to raise them and call them hers."

Her words hit like a truck, slicing through me before I had a chance to process. My heart plummeted.

"What? That's a lie!" I yelled, my voice cracking under the weight of my own doubt.

"Lie?" Lola mocked, cackling like she was high off nitrous oxide. "Ask the bitch yourself. Zalo's been messing with one of those hoes in Mcculloh Homes for years. His sisters last two kids—They're his. Unlike you, I do my research. Check his phone. Stupid bitch."

Her words were too detailed to ignore. Zalo definitely spent a lot of time out Mcculloh Homes. And how the fuck did she know anything about all Pita's kids? It all made too much sense. My body felt heavy, anger bubbling up until I couldn't hold it in anymore.

Before I knew it, I charged her, fists flying.

*T*he ride to Carmen's house felt endless. My knuckles throbbed, and Lola's blood stained my shirt. My hands gripped the steering wheel, slick with sweat. Adrenaline coursed through me, battling with the anxiety that came from anticipating the truth.

When I burst into Carmen's house, she thought I was hurt at first. But when I stormed into Pita's room, they realized this wasn't about me—it was about them. Carmen stepped in front of her daughter, protective as any mother would be. But Pita? She folded like a lawn chair. She told me everything, down to the name of the mother. Two-year-old Zachariah, and one-year-old Maria weren't her kids. They were Zalo's. The plan had been for her to raise them as her own to protect Zalo's reputation and preserve his marriage.

The kids I'd loved on, bought birthday gifts for, and called niece and nephew were my husband's illegitimate children. My daughter's "cousins" were her brother and sister. I stared at Pita, disgusted. She'd been the butt of every joke for years, criticized for her choices. And all this time, she'd been covering for Zalo. I couldn't even look at Carmen. What kind of mother lets her son pawn his dirty ass ways on his younger sister? The whole family was pathetic. And I wasn't about to keep playing a role in their circus.

I grabbed my daughter and left. My heart was shattered, but I told myself one thing as I slammed the door behind me: I wasn't looking back.

KYSON MCCARTER

$\mathcal{I}$'d been on bullshit lately. The reason was because, 'no' was never an option for me. I had to switch up my strategy to get Easton to let her guard down. I was aggressive by nature, but she didn't always respond to that shit. For that reason, I had to tone it down at times. At the same time, I had to turn it up when it came to other shit. I believed in fate, but I also believed in making shit happen. Her flat tire. I'd paid a motherfucker to slice. Loco had known earlier that day that he was getting Easton's truck before she even knew she was going to have a flat. How convenient was it for me to be around after it happened to save the day?

I knew that the little nigga she was fucking with, was a busy nigga. He was a boss on a Lieutenant level, so he was running around babysitting and passing out work, while I was higher on the totem pole, and had other people handling shit for me.

While he would take decades to get to Easton in the event of a crisis, I was always available and one phone call away. Or somewhere lurkin. It depended on the day. I had more time on my hand lately since Kobra and I were playing the shadows. So much time that I had even convinced Tyra to help a nigga out.

My plan had worked, and sis was helping a nigga win over her homegirl. I'd done my research on Zalo and to be frank, the nigga wasn't shit. He took care of home, but he played in the streets and had some shady business practices. I wasn't perfect by a long shot but when it came to quality, I was certainly superior.

Tyra still refused my money but she would tip a nigga off on where Easton would be so I could conveniently breeze through. I didn't give a fuck about looking like no stalker ass nigga because when I wanted something, I was determined to get it. And when I got it, it was mine. I didn't give a fuck about no Zalo. Not now. Not ever.

"*L*et us help you," Tyra begged in the phone for the third time that day.

"I told you, I'm good. I'm going to figure everything out on my own."

After leaving Carmen's with my daughter, I picked up my son's remains and rolled out on Zalo. I'd been staying at my mom's house for the past week. Since then, I'd been depressed and confused about my next move. *Should I throw away everything I had with Zalo over mistakes he had made?* That was the question that clouded my thoughts most of the time. I was unsure how the hell having two babies outside of his marriage were mistakes. Sounded more like choices to me.

Zalo had been blowing my phone up and at the moment, I refused to talk to him. Not even about our daughter. Unlike the bum bitch he'd taken his two kids from, I was fully capable of caring for mine. Nevertheless, the nigga was still my husband so at some point, I planned to sit down and have a conversation with him. For now, I was dealing with living at my mom's temporarily and making the best out of the situation.

I had some money saved, so I'd taken off a few weeks from work to get my mind right and focus on Kyllie. She was having a hard time adjusting to the lack of space, as well as the living conditions. My mother still drank heavily, and most days was in a drunken stupor. I didn't even bother her with talks of getting sober, because I knew it was going to take more than a motivational speech for her to put down the bottle. There were days that my mother wouldn't move from a spot all day. I'd walk by her and she would reek of piss and shit. I'd clean her up but Kyllie being the nosy and inquisitive four-year-old, would still ask a million questions.

"Why does mommom smell like poop?"

"Why mommom got that big wet spot on her pants?"

"Did she pee herself?"

"Mommom won't play with me like Mommom Carmen."

While the house and my mother's behavior were normal for me, they weren't normal for a child like Kyllie. She was used to a different lifestyle. Used to different living conditions. The bathroom was deplorable when we got there. Kyllie cried and refused to touch anything, let alone sit down and relieve herself. Urine, as well as light streaks of shit coated the toilet; while the rest of the house was dusty and looked like it hadn't been swept or mopped in months. I blamed myself for not coming to check on her more. I couldn't help but blame Wave too. Despite our childhood, that was still our mom and we should've been looking out for her more. I made a vow that when I got out of there, I would stop by more and help her out. Help clean up and try to get the house up to par. I drove around in a Mercedes. That was the least I could do.

Kyllie and I had settled in my old room. With a clean comforter, some fresh linen and a wipe down, it was decent enough to sleep in. The first night, while Kyllie slept, I stayed up all night cleaning and bringing the house up to a satisfactory level. There was still a lot of work to do so I knew that most of the house would be restricted to her.

I'd been sitting in my thoughts for nearly a week and I was ready to become proactive. I planned to meet with some contractors and start making larger repairs to the house. I couldn't lie, being back at my mother's house had humbled me in so many ways. It reminded me of what and where I came from. I'd been doing what people considered well while with Zalo, but truth was, none of that success was my own. It was all his. When it was all said and done, I had nothing but my hustle.

"Girl, I'm not trying to talk down on your mom's house or anything, but you can't stay there. Shit done got bad over there. Come stay with me. Go stay with Wave. Hell, go stay with Miracle. Her neighborhood ain't shit either, but yo' mama's raggedy ass house ain't it."

Tyra's voice reminded me that I was on the phone with her.

"Tyra please. You're so dramatic. We grew up around here. These people know me. I'll be just fine."

Tyra huffed in defeat.

"Alright girl. When you come to your senses, you know where I keep my spare. You're welcome anytime. And make sure you keep your phone charged. I need to make sure I know where you are at all times," she said seriously.

I chuckled. When I told everyone that I would be staying at my mom's, they demanded I share my location. Her house was in Sandtown and it was bad. I knew that but I didn't plan to be there long.

"Stop worrying. I will."

"Okay, well I love you. You be safe."

"I love you too."

We ended the call with the unspoken expectation that we would talk to each other tomorrow.

~

*A*n hour had passed, Kyllie was sleep, and I was leaning against the wall while she lay against me. The tv was off and all I could do was sit in my thoughts. I still had so many questions about Lola's accusations.

Why did he take that girl's kids like that? Who was she? Why was Lola so spiteful and vengeful?

I couldn't help but think about how life would be if

I didn't go back to Zalo. I'd really have to step my game up if I wanted to maintain Kyllie's quality of living. Maybe I could open my own shop. Rent out some suites. Move further out near the beach. My grandmother used to take my mama and her siblings to Ocean City when they were growing up. My mama loved the beach and had actually named Wave from the ripples of the ocean. I'd been named Easton because she often spent some time in a small town of the same name with some of her cousins when she was younger.

My mama had a decent life because her mama had worked hard to give it to her. Even making sure they had a forever home by purchasing the house. I wanted that for Kyllie, and I couldn't keep relying on her daddy to ensure that. I had to be the one to do so. I remembered how I had turned my hustle up at the tender age of fourteen for Quan. I had to do the same for Kyllie.

The flash of headlights snapped me out of my thoughts. I frowned, watching the glow cut across the room through the edges of the curtains. My mama's house was smack in the middle of a row of mostly abandoned homes. Nobody just pulled up around here. The little bit of folks that lived on the block were elderly, didn't have vehicles, or hardly had company.

I slid Kyllie off me gently, easing her onto the bed and tucking the blanket around her. She murmured something but didn't wake. I wasn't worried about her waking up. She was early to bed and early to rise. Quietly, I stood and crept to the window. The sheet we used to cover the cracked blinds was thick but flimsy enough to let some light through

I pulled the edge of the blind back and peered out. My heart skipped. A black Lamborghini Urus sat idle on the curb. Kyson.

I held my breath as the driver's door opened, and he stepped out, his tall frame illuminated by the street-light. He moved like he had all the time in the world, his confidence cutting through the chill of the night. He was bundled up. Wearing a shiny black coat and a skully, his braids peeking through the bottom.

"Damn it," I muttered under my breath, pulling away from the window. My heart thudded, and for a moment, I didn't know what to do.

I wasn't ready to face him, but before I could talk myself out of it, my feet were moving. I tiptoed down-stairs, careful not to wake my mama, who was passed out on the couch. Six empty beer cans were scattered on the floor around her, the smell of alcohol faint but familiar. I shook my head, biting back a sigh. That could wait. My nightgown swayed as I continued to walk. When I reached the door, my chest was tight, my palms sweaty. I opened it slowly, just as Kyson raised his hand to knock.

"Wassup, E," he said, his voice low and smooth. His smirk was effortless, the kind that could knock you off your game if you let it.

"What are you doing here?" I asked, gently nudging him back, stepping out and pulling the door closed behind me.

His eyes flicked down. "You out here barefoot?" He licked his lips and then openly admired my half-exposed body in the nightie I wore. It was expensive but still thin, stopping mid-thigh.

I looked down at my toes, wiggling them against the cold concrete porch. "Does it matter?" I said, crossing my arms. "Why are you here?"

"I came to check on you," he said, leaning casually against the porch railing. "Haven't seen you at the shop. Tried to book with you, but your books were closed. You good?"

"Yeah, I'm fine," I said quickly. Too quickly.

His eyebrow lifted slightly, but he didn't press. "You don't look fine," he said, slowly peering around the neighborhood.

"I'm just dealing with some personal shit. Needed a break." I admitted. "How'd you know I'd be here?" I asked, my tone sharper than I intended.

"You told me," he said, his voice even. He hid it well, but I could tell that he was lying like shit. "That day your tire blew. You mentioned you were from Sand-town. I know a few niggas out here. I asked around. People know your mom. It wasn't hard to figure out."

I folded my arms tighter, the chill seeping into my skin.

"Relax," he said, chuckling. "I'm not a stalker. Come on, let's grab something to eat.

"At seven at night?" I asked.

"Yeah," he chuckled. "Ain't no time limit on eating."

I can't leave," I said. "My daughter's upstairs, and my

mom—" I cut myself off. No need to go into details. "I can't leave.

"That's cool," he said, nodding toward the truck. "Then just come sit with me. Get warm. It's cold and you don't have on any clothes, out here trembling and shit." He was right. My lip quivered from the cold breeze whipping against my body. He pulled off his coat and tossed it around me. I hesitated but eventually followed him, my steps unsure. The second I slid into the passenger seat, the heat hit me. His cologne lingered, warm and spicy, filling the space between us.

For a while, we just talked. About everything and nothing. Kyson had this way of making me forget how fucked up everything was, even if just for a little while. He always talked like shit was so easy. Like it could be.

"Tell me your story," he said after a moment of silence.

I wasn't sure what he meant. My brow rose in confusion. I turned to him for clarity.

"What do you mean?"

"What stole your spirit? I can tell there was once a light inside of you; yet on the outside you show darkness. Pain. What happened? I mean, I see where you come from, but I know a lot of people from the hood and it takes more than some living conditions to steal your joy. It's something else. I can look in your eyes and tell there used to be a spark there. But it's been replaced by sadness."

A wave of emotions washed over me. My lip trembled and then the wall that I had placed up, immediately crumbled. I buried my face in my hands and began weeping. I felt Kyson's arm wrap around me and pull me into him. We stayed that way for the next ten minutes.

Kyson could read people very well so I knew there was no reason to hide my emotions. He made it safe to be vulnerable and that's what I needed. I needed to let it out. I needed the strength of a man to hold me up. Tell me it would be okay and tell me in a way that I actually believed it.

"You ready to talk?" he asked softly. I nodded and went to speak but grief paralyzed my vocal chords.

"I lost my son in a car accident," I finally choked out. "He was speeding and flipped his car on the expressway." I began sobbing again while Kyson stroked my back.

I didn't say another word. My cries told him everything. I hoped so anyway. I didn't need to say that I was crushed. That I questioned my existence. That I felt guilty. I didn't need to say that the loss of my son had devastated me and taken away most of the light I'd carried.

It felt good to let it out. To grieve without feeling guilty about doing so. I cried for nearly an hour and Kyson didn't say a word. He just held me and let me be. When I was done, we just sat. Until he decided to share with me that he had lost his mother. Unlike my son, his mother's death had come violently.

"I was angry for a long time, and I remember everyone telling me to "man up". That life had to go on.

I hated hearing that shit. I'd never tell anybody that shit. Grief is forever. It's been over twenty years and I still get emotional thinking about her."

I looked at him. "Really."

He nodded. Then his hand brushed my thigh. It wasn't intentional at first, just a casual movement as he adjusted in his seat. But when he didn't move it away, the air shifted.

"You alright?" he asked, his voice low.

I nodded, though my throat felt tight. His fingers traced slow circles against my skin, his touch light but deliberate. My breath hitched, my body betraying me.

"I don't know who told you had to be, but around me, you don't have to be tough all the time, E," he murmured. "Let me take care of you, even if just for a little while."

His words melted something in me, and before I could think twice, I leaned toward him. Our lips met, hesitant at first, then deeper, hungrier. I didn't know if it was all the emotions that I was feeling or if because I really wanted to get back at Zalo, but I wanted Kyson. I climbed onto his lap, straddling him. His hands gripped my waist, pulling me closer as the heat between us built, consuming everything else.

"Kyson," I whispered against his lips, my voice trembling. Apprehension had overcome me. I had lit a fire. Thrown gasoline on it actually and no longer could control it. I wanted to back out, but I was too far. He wasn't going to let me.

"Shh," he said, his lips trailing down my neck. "I got you."

My resolve crumbled. Kyson hiked up my nightgown and pulled my panties to the side, easing a finger inside of me. I gasped. He fingered me gently as I leaned into him, gently dipping my tongue in and out of his mouth and sucking his bottom lip into mine.

"Mmmm," I groaned into his mouth.

My body was swelling with desire and anticipation. Kyson pulled his finger out and used his mouth to suck off all my juices. He grinned as my adrenaline went wild. Pulling down my nightie, he exposed one of my breasts, tonguing and tasting it hungrily. While he made slow circles around my areola, I moaned some more. Pulling away from my breast, he whispered in my ear.

"Can I have some of you?"

His words. The request. My pussy felt like it was about to exploded. I nodded desperately.

"Yes."

I didn't know what the hell I was thinking. What I was doing. But I kept going. I helped Kyson unbuckle his pants and after a brief struggle, freed his thick, long, caramel colored dick. It was beautiful. Just like him. I wanted to do more. Explore every inch of him but there was no room. There was no time. Instead, I leaned up and eased down onto him. He slid inside of me while I moaned. My walls stretching to accommodate his girth.

When he was fully inside of me, my body bucked,

and I slowly began to ride him. Up and down. Down and up. He wrapped his hands around my waist as our bodies became familiar with one another. My pussy cried creamy tears of pleasure. He felt so good. So many feelings were going through me. Marriage. Baby carriage. The sky was the limit for us.

I was in a trance. My curls bounced freely as I rolled my head around in bliss. I'd had my share of lovers but none of them had ever made me feel this way. None of them had ever felt this way. Or fit perfectly.

Kyson groaned and leaned my body closer to his, running his tongue up and down the side of my neck. Kyson was the remedy my wounded soul desperately needed. Zalo was my man ... but he didn't fucking compare.

The windows fogged, the truck rocking as we moved together, the world outside disappearing. I didn't care about anything else. Not Zalo, not my mama's mess waiting for me back inside. For once, I let myself feel. Be. Enjoy.

After we climaxed, we stayed there for a moment, breathing hard, Kyson's arms wrapped around me.

"I like you E." He kissed me softly. I want to help you," he said. "First thing's first, you can't be out here living like this," he said. "Let me help you."

I knew he didn't mean it in a critical way. He was just concerned. Everyone was. What they was saying was true. Most of the houses were boarded up. Windows broken. Trash strewn everywhere. And the gun violence in the neighborhood was an entire story of its own. Weekly homicides were common.

"I don't need your help," I said, shaking my head. "I'll figure everything out."

I was still straddled on top of him. Titty and ass out. Head nestled into his.

He chuckled, his breath warm against my cheek. "You're stubborn, you know that?"

Before I could respond, the screech of tires cut through the quiet night. My heart sank as a familiar red Audi pulled up, its doors flying open. Zalo and two of his goons jumped out, their faces twisted with anger. Zalo yanked the driver side door open, grabbing me by the hair and pulling me out of the truck. While my body and feet scraped against the ground, one of Zalo's homies ran up on Kyson, shoving a gun with a drum against his temple.

"You thought I was stupid?" Zalo spat. His eyes burned with fury as he looked between us. "Bitch, what I tell you? You 'bout to die right beside this nigga!"

To be continued.

ABOUT THE AUTHOR

"Where rebellion meets romance. Crafting stories for the women who make their own rules."

Shontaiye Moore was born and raised on the Eastern Shore in Salisbury, Maryland. Daughter to an avid reader, her love for literature developed at a young age with the Berenstain Bears and Goosebumps books. She now writes Black Women's Fiction and Urban Romance, where her stories demonstrate relatable struggles, rebellious women, and most importantly, the power and rewards of love. Armed with a B.S. in Business, she writes full-time. When she isn't writing, she's studying for her Master's In Data Science and spending time with her daughter Tatyana aka Toots. Follow her on all social media platforms.